SOPHIE PITT-TU
DISCOVERS AN

Dyan Sheldon says that her writing for young adults
"comes from personal experience. I just make the
characters younger. I thought I would outgrow these
experiences – but they keep happening." She is the
author of many books for young people, including
*Confessions of a Teenage Drama Queen*; *My Perfect
Life*; *The Boy of My Dreams*; *Tall, Thin and Blonde*;
*And Baby Makes Two*; *Planet Janet*; and a number of
stories for younger readers. She also writes books for
adults. American by birth, Dyan Sheldon lives in north
London.

Books by the same author

*And Baby Makes Two*
*The Boy of My Dreams*
*Confessions of a Teenage Drama Queen*
*My Perfect Life*
*Planet Janet*
*Tall, Thin and Blonde*
*Undercover Angel*
*Undercover Angel Strikes Again*

# Sophie Pitt-Turnbull discovers AMERICA

# DYAN SHELDON

WALKER BOOKS
AND SUBSIDIARIES
LONDON · BOSTON · SYDNEY · AUCKLAND

First published 2003 by Walker Books Ltd
87 Vauxhall Walk, London SE11 5HJ

2 4 6 8 10 9 7 5 3 1

Text © 2003 Dyan Sheldon
Cover illustration © 2003 Phil Hankinson

This book has been typeset in Countryhouse and Sabon

Printed in Great Britain by Cox & Wyman Ltd,
Reading, Berkshire

British Library Cataloguing in Publication Data:
a catalogue record for this book
is available from the British Library

ISBN 0-7445-8326-8

www.walkerbooks.co.uk

# Contents

# Me

I've always known exactly who I am. I am Sophie Pitt-Turnbull. I live with Mummy, Daddy and my older brother, Xar, in a terraced house in Putney, London, England. Daddy writes books (novels and biographies) and Mummy is a housewife and painter (portraits of domestic animals). Although Daddy's family didn't begin to prosper until the Industrial Revolution, Mummy can trace her ancestors back to Henry II, so I was raised with a strong sense of tradition and history. "Never forget that you're British," Nana Bea likes to say, and I never have. I've always been happy with who I am. Not in a stuck-up, I'm-the-best-thing-that's-happened-since-the-invention-of-the-light-bulb  sort of way, of course. More in a God's-done-a-lot-worse-than-Sophie-Pitt-Turnbull sort of way. Even after Jocelyn Scolfield said all that stuff about me being a bit on the dull and passive side, I was still satisfied with myself. I reckoned that I'd improve with age (like wine or cheese), but I never actually expected to *change*. Not change so much that I could divide my life into two parts: the part with the *old me* and the part with the *new me*. But I never expected to discover America either, so that isn't surprising.

# After Eight Hundred Years My Family Decides to Break with Tradition

Daddy always says that one can't really complain about one's life unless one lives in a cardboard box in Somalia or somewhere like that, but by the middle of last year I was beginning to disagree. I had clean drinking water and food and loos and all that sort of thing, of course, but that didn't mean I didn't know what it is to suffer. I knew. The past six months had taught me that one can suffer just as much on three meals a day as on none (except that one's not hungry all the time). I was having a truly *ghastly* time. *Ghastly* as in beginning to feel a bit sorry for myself. Indeed, it was so ghastly that I was actually looking forward to spending the summer in the cottage in France for the first time since I was ten – the year all my friends went to Disney World.

And then I was having a cup of tea in the kitchen one afternoon while Mummy was getting supper ready, and I said, "Isn't it time we did our shopping for the hols?" Our pre-holiday shop was one of my favourite traditions.

Mummy didn't look up from the chicken she was stuffing. "Pardon?" she asked.

"It *is* the middle of June," I reminded her. "There are only a few weeks left."

And that was when Mummy said (and I quote), "What are you on about, Sophie? We're not going to France this year. I thought you understood that."

I didn't understand that at all. Nobody had bothered to tell *me*. And now that they had, I was *aghast*. There's no other word for it. *Aghast* as in why did everything happen to me? I mean, it wasn't as if I'd done anything wrong.

"But we always go to France for the summer." We'd been doing it since before I was born, for heaven's sake. "It's a family tradition."

"Well, this year we're starting a new tradition." Mummy lifted the chicken into the roasting pan. "This summer we're staying in London."

Of all the summers for this to happen, it would have to be this one, wouldn't it?

"But we can't!" I may actually have wailed.

Mummy wanted to know why we couldn't stay in London. There were several reasons why.

"Because everybody else is going away, that's why," I told her. "I'll be all on my own for the entire summer."

This was the first reason.

"Jocelyn's not going away," said Mummy.

**10**

Jocelyn had been my best friend since the start of secondary school – and the other five hundred reasons why I couldn't stay in Putney. She was also the major reason I was having such a phenomenally bad year.

In the past six months, Jocelyn Scolfield had lost the following: my mobile phone, two films we'd rented on my parents' card from the video shop, and three books I'd taken out of the school library. She'd also told her mother it was my fault the loo flooded the bathroom like that (thank God they were insured!), wrecked my bicycle (thank God we were insured!) and stolen my boyfriend (Jocelyn said she didn't steal Daniel; she said he jumped ship because he found me "a bit on the dull and passive side" – which I reckoned was a classic example of blaming the victim).

Because of my ancestry I'd inherited a very resilient nature, of course, so I'd forgiven Jocelyn for all those things, and we were still friends. On the other hand, Jocelyn and Daniel were the only ones of our group who were staying in Putney over the hols, and I really didn't want to spend the summer watching them see how far down each other's throats they could get their tongues. Not that Mummy knew any of that. It wasn't the sort of thing we discussed. The Pitt-Turnbulls are very private people.

Mummy said there were *extenuating circumstances* that made going to France impossible. *Extenuating circumstances* as in Nana Bea, my

11

brother, Xar, and Daddy. Nana Bea had done something to her back chasing a fox out of her garden and needed Mummy to run errands for her. Xar had returned from his gap year in India in a mood and wanted to go to Cuba, not France. Daddy had a book to finish.

I tried to reason with Mummy. I pointed out that the doctors couldn't find anything wrong with Nana Bea's back, so she was probably just carrying on about it to get sympathy. And even if it did hurt as much as she said, she could always pay someone to do her shopping and go to the cash machine for her while we were away. I further pointed out that Xar had been alone with India for nearly a year without wrecking it, so I didn't see why he couldn't be left on his own with the house for a few weeks. And I reminded her that Daddy always had a book he had to finish.

To which brilliant arguments Mummy replied (and again I quote), "No, not on your life, and this time Daddy is really behind." (There was more, of course. At least half an hour of *what if?* What if Nana Bea got worse while we were away? What if Xar burnt down the house with his incense and his candles and his God knows what? What if there was an accident on the way to France and the disk and the laptop with Daddy's book on it were destroyed?)

I was *devastated* – there's no other word for it. *Devastated* as in I couldn't believe how God had it in for me all of a sudden.

I begged and I pleaded.

I tried to bribe Xar into saying he'd go to France after all.

I wept and I sulked.

I asked Daddy to intervene.

I spent two days at home with the headache from hell.

Xar told me to do something disgusting to myself and Daddy told me to talk to my mother.

Mummy told me to put a sock in it.

The only person who showed me any sympathy was our cleaner, Maria. She brought me one of her magic potions disguised as soup for my headache and asked me what was wrong. I don't usually speak to Maria very much because her accent's very strong and I'm not always certain what we're talking about, but in my weakened condition I told her about being *devastated* because we were staying in Putney all summer. Maria said I should talk to God. Maria talks to God all the time. I tried to explain that we're C of E and don't really go in for that sort of thing. Daddy says we're latent Christians (we believe in God and He believes in us, but we don't really bother each other). Maria said that one's meant to bother God. What else does He have to do all day?

So I told God that if He'd get me out of Putney even for just a few weeks I'd do volunteer work for Friends of the Earth all winter, which I reckoned He'd appreciate, since it is His planet, after all.

There was no response from God at first.

Maria said that was normal. She said God wasn't a cash machine – one couldn't expect instant results. Instead Maria started bothering God on my behalf. She even lit candles.

And *it worked*! (All I can say is, thank God I'm not an atheist. They don't know what they're missing.)

On 2 July Mummy talked to Jacqueline Salamanca on the telephone. Jacqueline Salamanca is Mummy's American chum from art school. They haven't seen each other since they were young and didn't have to think about hormone replacement therapy, but every year Mummy rings Jacqueline to wish her a happy birthday. Fortunately, this wasn't one of the traditions Mummy decided she could live without. Somewhere in this conversation Jacqueline Salamanca said that her eldest daughter (Cherry) was driving her mad because she wanted to go to Europe that summer and couldn't – and Mummy said that her only daughter (me) was driving her mad because she wanted to go anywhere that wasn't London.

And then (out of the blue) Jacqueline Salamanca said why didn't they swap daughters until school started? Mummy said she'd talk it over with me.

"You don't have to say yes," said Mummy. "I know you have your heart set on getting out of London for the summer, but I really want you to give this some thought. It's not like going to France, you know. If you decide you don't like it when you get there, you can't just turn round and take the next train home."

There was more, of course. What if the plane crashed? What if it was hijacked? What if something dreadful happened to me because Mummy wasn't there to keep an eye on me? What if I didn't get on with the Salamancas? What if I was allergic to the New York air? What if I didn't like the food? What if I became ill? What if...? What if...? What if...? What if...?

I said it was a wonder she wasn't the writer, given her imagination.

But although I pooh-poohed all of Mummy's worries, I have to admit that if this offer had been made the year before I would probably have said no. I'd never been away from home before (unless you count overnight and school trips and things like that, which I don't). Going so far away all on my own was a little scary – especially to America, which Nana Bea still insists on calling the Wild West. And as Daddy said when he finally heard about it, "Crossing the pond isn't like crossing the Channel, is it?"

But this wasn't the year before, and a part of me wanted to prove that I wasn't as dull and passive as some people might think. I was going to be brave, bold and intrepid. I was going to have a real adventure – and possibly get a new boyfriend and best friend to boot. Besides, it wasn't as if I'd be living in a youth hostel without knowing a soul in the country – I'd be living with a personal friend of Mummy's and her children in an artistic but family environment. It was perfect. I felt that despite all the bad things that were constantly happening, God really did know what He was doing.

As soon as Mummy rang Jacqueline back to tell her it was a done deal, I wrote out a cheque for Friends of the Earth and took it down to the postbox at the corner. I told God to consider it a thank-you note.

I didn't know then that God wasn't through with me yet.

# I Get a Lot of Information about America – of Which Only Two Pieces Will Actually Do Me Any Good

Just about everyone I knew either had been to America or knew someone who had (even Maria has a cousin in New Jersey).

There were quite a few horror stories.

There were crocodiles in the sewers and sewage in the drinking water. Everybody was armed and ready to fire. Most New Yorkers were mugged at least twice every year. Janice Freestone's cousin had spent a summer in New York when at least three babies were shot in their cots, and her uncle had worked with a businessman who was gunned down making a phone call on the street. Sanjay Puli's uncle worked near a restaurant where one of the waiters had once blown away a diner. Evan Skeller's grandfather had met a cab driver who'd been hijacked in broad daylight. A friend of Abbie Maidston's father had got lost in somewhere called the Bronx and was lucky to be alive.

But it wasn't all gloom and doom.

Janice Freestone's aunt said that although it could get quite hot and I'd need a real summer wardrobe, everyone had air conditioning, so it was a good idea to pack a warm jumper as well.

Milla Hewitt said that Americans loved to power dress and only liked new things, so I should make sure I took enough clothes so I didn't have to wear anything more than twice. Milla also said that everything in America was much cheaper than in Britain, so I should plan to do a lot of shopping. Milla recommended Fifth Avenue – Fifth Avenue made Oxford Street look like Shepherd's Bush market.

Amy Lawson said I was about to discover how completely *boring* and old hat London was. She said I wouldn't believe how exciting New York was. Especially the art scene. Amy said there was always something going on – openings and parties and things like that – so I should probably do a lot of sleeping before I went because it was going to be all systems go once I got to New York. Amy reckoned that since Mummy's friend was an artist she was bound to live in a loft in SoHo – possibly with a view of the Empire State Building. According to Amy, most New York artists not only lived in SoHo but had weekend houses in the Hamptons (an exclusive beach community absolutely packed with celebrities). Amy advised me to make sure I had enough casual outfits for barbecues and sailing and tennis, as well as cocktail dresses, et cetera, for New York.

Polly Matthewman said I'd also need state-of-the-art trainers and at least two tracksuits, because New Yorkers spent their weekends running round Central Park carrying weights and listening to their Discmans. She said it was a really good way to meet the right sort of men. Polly had dated a law student she'd met when he knocked her down because she wasn't looking where she was going. (He'd thought she might sue him – Americans are *always* suing someone, aren't they? – but she settled for dinner.)

Alison Flaxman said that even though New Yorkers always wore baseball caps, chewed gum and didn't speak a second language, they were more sophisticated than Europeans.

Gemma Bloom once stayed with her mother's cousin in Scarsdale (an exclusive community nowhere near the beach and absolutely packed with professionals), and based on her experience Gemma reckoned that Cherry Salamanca's room would be at least twice the size of mine – and she'd not only have her own phone and bathroom with a power shower, she'd probably have her own digital telly and possibly a fridge too (all things Gemma's room in Scarsdale had).

Everyone agreed that New Yorkers were the most positive and energetic people going. Especially the men. New York men made London men look like children (and unattractive ones at that). New York men, though sensitive, were so much more masculine and aggressive that it was hard to believe they

19

belonged to the same species. Polly said that was why Americans thought most British men were gay.

By the time the day of my departure arrived I felt I knew so much about America I was practically an honorary citizen.

Mummy, of course, didn't agree. As far as Mummy was concerned I might as well have been the first white person ever to set foot on North American soil. She appeared at my door as I was checking my packing list for the last time.

Mummy smiled. "Don't you look nice."

I couldn't have agreed more. I was wearing a new white-on-white summer dress with a matching jacket, new white high-heeled sandals and a straw hat with tiny pink roses round the brim.

"I just wanted to have a quick chat with you before we set off," she said.

"Now?" I glanced at my watch. "But we have to go."

"It'll only take a few minutes."

I'd packed away all my personal possessions and put them in the loft – with the exception of my stuffed animals, because I reckoned they made the room look homely and also because I didn't like the idea of them being in boxes all summer. Mummy shoved Mr Wiggle and the Three Little Pigs over and sat down on the edge of my bed. "Why don't you come and sit next to me?"

"But I haven't even locked my bag yet."

Mummy patted the spot beside her. "Please."

It was then that I noticed the packet in her

hands. It had to be a present. She'd already given me her credit card to use for emergencies and my new suitcase, so I reckoned it must be the digital camera I'd asked for. I sat down.

Mummy said she just wanted me to know how much she and Daddy loved me.

I said I knew that, but at the moment I really wanted to finish my packing.

Mummy said that because they loved me they were going to worry about me – all by myself three thousand miles away in a foreign country.

I reminded her that I wasn't going to be by myself.

She said I still had to be *prepared*. (Mummy likes to be prepared for every possible situation. Daddy says that why she has so much trouble doing anything.)

I said that I had sixteen pairs of socks and twenty knickers in my case – how much more prepared could I be?

She said she wanted to be sure I understood that New York wasn't Putney.

I said I didn't think I'd confuse them. I reckoned the Empire State Building and the yellow cabs would be dead giveaways.

Mummy said, "No, really."

She wanted my solemn promise that I wouldn't go out on the street without Mrs Salamanca.

I promised.

And I was definitely not to ride on the tube by myself – there were gangs on the tube.

I asked her gangs of what, but it didn't lighten her mood.

"Under no circumstances are you to go out on your own at night. Not even down to the corner shop. It's much too dangerous."

"I won't," I said. "Not even if the flat's on fire." I started to get up.

She pulled me back down. "And you are not to speak to strangers."

I was tempted to point out that since it was a foreign country they were all going to be strangers, but I didn't want to get into an argument right then – the last thing I wanted was to miss the plane.

I said that I wouldn't, not even if they spoke to me first.

"I'm not asking you to be rude," said Mummy. "Just cautious. And don't loiter on the street either. America has a lot of drive-by shootings and psychopaths."

Daddy called up from the front hall. "You just about ready, Sophie? You want a hand with your bag?"

Mummy thrust the packet at me. "I talked Dr Giles into giving me double your usual prescriptions for your headache and allergy pills, so you should have enough. And I've put some multiple vitamins in there as well – I'm not certain Americans understand about nutrition."

"Thanks. Just what I wanted."

"Sometimes it's better to get what you need rather than what you want," said Mummy.

"I know," I said. "I really am grateful."

"Now, if you do run out you're to go to a doctor immediately. I've put the insurance forms in your hand luggage so you can fill them out straight away if you have to."

"Thank you. I'll do that."

"And you've got the credit card, but write the number down somewhere safe in case you mislay it."

"I've already done that. It's in my address book."

She patted my hand. The only time I'd ever seen her eyes mist over like that was when she was peeling onions. "We're going to miss you."

"I'm going to miss you too."

Mummy stood up so quickly I nearly fell off the bed. "I'll get your father."

"Good God!" said Daddy when he came into the room. "Is that a suitcase or a trunk?"

I said I had to fit everything in, didn't I? He wouldn't want me putting things in cardboard boxes like some sort of refugee, would he?

"Catherine of Braganza didn't bring this many clothes with her when she came here to marry Charles II," he said.

He grabbed hold of my case and rolled it across the room, but when he got to the door he stopped and turned round.

"You will watch out for yourself, won't you, Sophie? All the way over there across the pond."

I said Mummy had already briefed me.

"And besides," I said, "it's not like it really is a

23

foreign country, is it, Daddy? I mean, really, it's about as foreign as Kingston – they do use cutlery and speak English."

This was when he gave me one of the two pieces of useful information I received.

"Best not forget that Britain and America are two countries separated by a common language."

# Things Start to Go Wrong

The long journey across the Atlantic gave me time to think and reflect – as countless other intrepid adventurers must have done while gazing at the empty sky (especially when they didn't have personal stereos or tellies to help while away the hours).

I began to see that if there was any truth to the claim that I occasionally tended to be a bit on the dull and passive side, it was completely the fault of Daddy and Mummy. They'd been smothering me with love and terror since I was born. They'd been protecting me into a coma. Especially Mummy – Mummy really does worry about *everything*.

By the time we landed at JFK I was wondering why I hadn't done something like this sooner. For the first time in sixteen years I was about to *really live* – free of Mummy's fretting and fussing. I was like Columbus – brave, bold and determined as I sailed into a whole new world. I was so excited

I would have run from the plane if my new shoes hadn't already been *killing* me and I hadn't been stuck at the end of a very slow-moving queue.

I was reminded of the millions of films I'd seen of hopeful immigrants arriving in America with all their possessions in their arms as I followed the throng of people into passport control (though none of them were carrying cloth sacks or anything like that, of course). The noise ... the confusion ... the pushing and shoving and whining children – this was what it was like.

When the woman who checked my documents told me to have a nice day, I smiled back and said, "You have a nice day too."

I was humming that song about New York being so good they named it twice as I followed the signs to collect my bag. This was how new lives began.

It was another forty-five minutes before I realized that it wasn't only how new lives began – it was how disasters began as well.

I stood beside the luggage carousel from the moment the first bag came out till the last bag was revolving round and round all by itself like an abandoned child, but my suitcase *never appeared.*

I was *stunned. Stunned* as in for God's sake – what was I meant to do without my *clothes*? My only consolation was that I had my toiletries and medication, et cetera, in my hand luggage (except, of course, for my razor, because of terrorists – that had to go in my bag in case I decided to run

26

amok with my Lady Gillette).

I told the woman at customer services that I didn't understand how they could have lost my bag. After all, I saw it go down the ramp with my own eyes. She said (and I quote), "But did you see it come out?" She assured me that they hadn't really lost my case – they'd just misplaced it. She took Mrs Salamanca's details and promised to ring as soon as they worked out where it was.

The Salamancas had been waiting ages for me by then, and I knew that if Mrs Salamanca was anything like Mummy she'd be beside herself with worry. I raced to the arrivals hall, rehearsing my apologies as I went.

The Salamancas weren't there. I was *baffled*. *Baffled* as in what was wrong with this picture? How could they not be there? After all, it wasn't as if they didn't know I was coming. Mummy even sent them a recent photo so they wouldn't have to do anything embarrassing like hold up a sign. And I knew what they looked like, because Mummy had a picture of all four of them sitting in front of a Christmas tree. (They were dressed like elves, but I reckoned I would still recognize them without the hats and ears as I am the daughter of an artist, after all.)

Once I was absolutely certain that the Sala-mancas weren't among the mob of people waving and shouting in the waiting area, I went to the information desk to see if they'd left a message for me. This was what Mummy would have done. But it was clearly not what Mrs Salamanca had done. I made the clerk check twice.

It was just as well I'd decided to be brave, bold and determined or I might have begun to panic a bit. Mummy, of course, had made sure I had some American money on me – just in case. I found a working payphone and rang the Salamancas'. The message on our answering machine at home is Daddy saying, "You've reached the Pitt-Turnbull residence; there is no one available to take your call. Please leave your number." The message on the Salamancas' machine was someone more or less shouting, "There's nobody here but us chickens" to some sort of extremely loud music.

There was nothing to do but wait. Despite the threat of drive-by shootings, I decided I had more chance of being spotted if I stood outside.

Good God, I thought as I stepped through the doors. No wonder Janice Freestone's aunt still talks about her summer in New York. The heat and noise hit me like an articulated lorry. It felt like I'd walked into an oven – one in which every car for miles was honking its horn. I could actually *see* the air. I positioned myself near the kerb – keeping a tight hold on my hand luggage and one eye out for fast-moving vehicles – and faced straight ahead so that no one would bother me.

Hours passed. Two policemen, three cleaners and a shady-looking character with a tattoo of that dead revolutionary with the beard and beret on his arm asked me if I was all right. Politely but firmly

I said that I was fine and that I was waiting for my friends.

But the truth was, I really couldn't understand how they could be so late. Mummy always allows extra time when she's meeting someone – in case she has a flat or the traffic's particularly awful – but even if Mrs Salamanca wasn't as sensible as Mummy, I reckoned she'd have to be coming from Alaska to take this long.

More hours went by. I was sweating so much I thought I was melting, and my feet were beginning to bleed. I could only pray I wasn't starting to pong as well. I began imagining all the dreadful things that might have happened to the Salamancas to delay them. What if they'd had a terrible accident? What if their car had broken down and the AA man couldn't fix it? Worse yet, what if their car had broken down and they'd been attacked by a psychopath or a drive-by shooter while they were waiting for the AA man?

I was about to go back inside to see if there was a message for me now, when my attention was caught by an extremely old van coming towards the terminal. It seemed to be smoking.

Not for one second did it occur to me that this van contained the Salamancas. I only stopped to look because the only time I've seen a car like that was one desperate night when there was nothing else on and Jocelyn and I watched that film *Woodstock*.

The van shuddered to a halt in front of me.

Quite a few arms suddenly started flapping out of the window and there was what Nana Bea would call a right ballyhoo coming from inside. I didn't see any guns, but I turned to retreat into the terminal just in case.

And that was when I heard the name "Soph!" being shouted behind me at a volume that would have summoned hounds. My name, of course, isn't Soph – it's Sophie, which is what *everyone* has always called me – but it was close enough to make me look round.

A rather mad-looking woman in a neon-orange jumpsuit with tiny Christmas trees swinging from her ears had leapt from the van and was hurtling towards me waving her hands. She had so much hair I would have thought she had a bush on her head if it hadn't been streaked with blue. I was *shocked*. There's no other word for it. *Shocked* as in frozen to the spot with a premonition of impending doom. All of Mummy's friends are very much like Mummy, but this person was *nothing* like Mummy – and I couldn't imagine that she ever had been – not even all those years ago when Mummy had long hair and went to pubs on a Saturday night. (Mummy did say that Jacqueline was quite a character – but everyone says that about Nana Bea too, and she doesn't wear orange jumpsuits and Christmas tree earrings in *July*.)

I said, "Mrs Salamanca?" as politely as some one struck numb with horror could.

She lunged for me, hugging me so tight I swear

she squeezed the sweat out of my clothes. I could hear the dripping as my feet left the pavement.

"I'm *so* sorry we're late," Mrs Salamanca bellowed in my ear. "We got so lost we would've wound up in New Jersey if we weren't surrounded by water."

Lost? I could hardly believe my ears. They hadn't been in an accident or attacked by a psychopath or had to wait half a lifetime for the AA to turn up – they'd got lost. I could just about accept that a busy airline could mislay a case – even one that was nearly the size of a trunk – but how could a person live in a city for decades and get lost going to the airport? It wasn't possible. I mean, they do have signs.

I disentangled myself from her bear-like embrace and started to apologize for causing her so much trouble, but Mrs Salamanca suddenly noticed that I didn't have any luggage. Mummy would have been absolutely distraught to hear that the airline had lost my case, but Mrs Salamanca just laughed.

"What a day!" She slapped me on the shoulder. "And it's not over yet."

I laughed along – but only because I didn't yet know how true those words were.

# Welcome to Brooklyn –
# So Good They Named It Once

Mrs Salamanca wrenched open the van's passenger door and introduced the two children who had been trying to climb out of the window.

"The one with the red hair is Gallup," she said. "And the one on top of him is Tampa."

The children I knew were called things like Jonathan and Eleanor, and they entered and left cars by doors.

"Oh," I murmured, "what unusual names."

Tampa informed me that they'd been named after the places where they were conceived. (It was just as well they weren't conceived in Wapping and Bath, if you ask me.)

I said, "Oh, like David Beckham's son."

Only Gallup had ever heard of David Beckham. "Isn't he the one they turned down for *The Simpsons* because he wasn't famous enough?" he asked.

The next few minutes were spent with Mrs Salamanca yelling (rather fruitlessly) at Gallup and

Tampa to get into the back so I could sit in the front with her.

People were starting to watch us.

"Really," I said, "if it's a problem I don't mind sitting in the back."

"Are you nuts?" When she really thought something was funny Mrs Salamanca's laugh sounded amazingly like the cry of a crane that's being strangled. "On the floor? In that lovely white dress?"

I glanced in the back, which was filled with all sorts of things (odd shoes, a couple of lamps, a bag of cement...) but nothing one could actually sit down on. I could see her point.

At last, after some more screaming and a lot of threats, Mrs Salamanca said, "In you go, Soph."

"Sophie," I grunted as I finally heaved myself into the passenger's side. Something fell off the dashboard, and the stuffing was coming out of the seat.

"You should hold on to something," Gallup advised me. "That seat belt's not great."

"Thank you," I said. "I'll do that."

"And watch out for the door," added Gallup. "Sometimes it opens."

"Isn't it meant to?" I joked.

"Not when you're moving."

I said I'd keep my eye on it.

Tampa wanted to know why I talked funny.

Mrs Salamanca sighed. "How many times do I have to tell you?" she shouted. "Soph comes from England. You know, like Harry Potter."

I opened my mouth to explain that everyone

33

called me Sophie, but I only got as far as "Actually" before Tampa cut me off.

"Are you a wizard?" she screamed in my ear.

If only.

Gallup wanted to know if I went to a school like Hogwarts. He wanted his own owl like Harry Potter, but Jake wouldn't let him have one.

I hadn't realized that Gallup and Tampa had a father – not one who lived with them – but I hid my surprise as the sound of rattling metal announced our departure from the kerb. I lunged forward and the seat belt undid itself. The door swung open when I let go to refasten it. I apologized for shrieking like that. Mrs Salamanca said she was used to it.

I reminded myself that resilience ran in my family and that nothing mattered next to the fact that I was spending the summer in *New York*. The obvious oddness of the Salamancas didn't matter – not even the possibility that I wouldn't live long enough to enjoy it mattered.

Mrs Salamanca talked to me non-stop as we belched and clattered out of JFK, while I held on tight to both the seat belt and the door and looked out of the window. Mrs Salamanca said the reason they'd got so lost was because she'd had a meeting with her landlord that had disoriented her. "You know what it's like," she said.

I didn't, of course – we've always owned our own home – but I said that I did to be polite.

Mrs Salamanca said that she had wanted to

throw me a little party so I could meet Cherry's friends, but except for Bachman they were all away. She said there were plenty of other kids my age in the neighbourhood and Mummy had told her I was good at making friends.

For at least ten minutes all I did was nod and say "Um" and "Oh?" and "Really?" and "That's perfectly fine."

And then I saw a sign with an arrow pointing right and the word MANHATTAN. We drove straight past it. I was beginning to understand how she got lost getting to the airport.

I broke into Mrs Salamanca's monologue as politely as I could to tell her that we'd missed our exit.

"Jake," screamed Mrs Salamanca.

For a second I thought she meant that her husband was standing at the side of the road thumbing a lift, but all I saw along the hard shoulder was rubbish.

"Pardon?"

"Jake!" she screamed again. "It's what everybody calls me."

I tried not to look appalled. I knew that women were often called by male names – Mummy had a friend named Sam, for heaven's sake – but I'd never called an adult by her first name unless it was preceded by the word "Aunt", and I had no intention of starting with Mrs Salamanca. (And I certainly wasn't about to call her Aunt, in case people thought we were related.)

I repeated that I thought we'd missed our exit.

"Why's that?" bellowed Mrs Salamanca.

I pointed behind us. "Because the sign for Manhattan was back there."

I was the only one who didn't laugh.

"But we don't live in Manhattan," honked Mrs Salamanca. "We live in Brooklyn."

It took me a few seconds to absorb this information. I reminded myself that I was a bold, brave and determined explorer. I was like Columbus – and like Columbus I'd apparently landed in the wrong place.

"Brooklyn?" Aside from it being the name of David Beckham's son (though I certainly wasn't about to bring that up again), the only thing I knew about Brooklyn was that a lot of gangster films were made there. I smiled at the Christmas trees swinging from her ears. "I'm sorry, I thought Mummy said that you lived in New York."

Tampa positioned her mouth next to my ear so I wouldn't miss a fraction of a decibel and shrieked, "We do live in New York, stupid. Brooklyn's part of New York."

I waited a few seconds for Mrs Salamanca to tell her off for calling me stupid, and when that didn't happen I said, "Well, I reckon I stand corrected."

Gallup said that I wasn't standing; I was sitting down. (If only just.)

Rather recklessly, I felt, Mrs Salamanca took a hand from the wheel to pat my knee. "Don't you worry, honey," she assured me, "you're going to *love* Brooklyn. It's got a lot more character than Manhattan."

I closed my eyes as we launched ourselves off the motorway – and when I opened them again we were on the set of a low-budget Mafia film. The buildings were run-down; the streets were dirty and grey. Seedy-looking blokes ran between the cars at the traffic lights selling air fresheners and roses. Brooklyn might have more character than Manhattan, but as far as I could see it was all bad. Brooklyn, I thought. So good they named it once.

By the time we finally pulled over to the kerb I was so shattered that I rather assumed something else had gone wrong. "What's the matter?" I asked. "Have we run out of petrol?" It certainly wouldn't have surprised me.

"What's petrol?" demanded Tampa.

Mrs Salamanca said it was gas. To me she said, "We're here! Home, sweet home!"

I looked at where we were. It was so *not* a SoHo loft that for a few seconds I still didn't understand what she meant.

Mrs Salamanca swung open her door and screamed, "This is it, Soph! The Casa Salamanca."

My eyes followed her pointing hand.

The Casa Salamanca was a small wooden house that didn't look as though it had been painted for at least twenty years. The front steps sagged and the railing was held together with duct tape. There were plants and fairy lights in every window and wind chimes made from stones and shells swung from the roof of the porch.

"Oh," I said as I clambered down from the van, "isn't it…" I searched for the right word. Odd? Unusual? Strange beyond belief? "Isn't it lovely." A row of small metal bats hung from the eaves; one of them seemed to be winking. "I've never seen anything quite like it before." That much was true – certainly not in real life – though I wouldn't have said that I felt I'd been missing a great deal.

"It's not much to look at, but it's home," said Mrs Salamanca as she marched towards the house. "Well, ours and the landlord's – so far."

Gallup and Tampa raced ahead of us. I took a step to follow them and tripped on the uneven pavement.

"It's my fault. I should've warned you." Mrs Salamanca helped me up. "You OK, Soph?"

"Sophie. Yes, I'm fine." I smiled. "I'm perfectly fine." I reached out for the railing that ran alongside the steps.

"Oh, don't hang on to that," warned Mrs Salamanca. "It's an accident waiting to happen. The landlord's too cheap to fix it. It's liable to come off in your hands." She took the house keys from the pocket of her jumpsuit. If the handbag industry depended on Mrs Salamanca for business it'd be bankrupt. "And watch yourself going into the house," she advised. "Pancho Villa likes to crap by the door."

By now I felt as though my smile was cemented

onto my face. "Oh, does he?" I didn't have the heart to ask who – or what – Pancho Villa was.

I stepped gingerly behind her, over the pile of cat poo in the hall, and right into a giant papier mâché fish that was hanging from the ceiling.

"Poor Soph," said Mrs Salamanca. "You don't have your sea legs yet, do you? Are you OK?"

"I'm fine." I rubbed my head. "I didn't expect anything to be hanging just there."

"You better not've broken my Chinese carp," warned Tampa.

"That's her costume for the Neptune Parade," Gallup explained.

I didn't ask what the Neptune Parade was either. I didn't want to know.

"So?" Mrs Salamanca gestured round the sitting room. "What do you think?"

I gazed about me, feeling dazed in more than one way and wondering what I could say that wouldn't sound rude.

There were things everywhere. Books, knick-knacks, pots, masks, pictures, boxes, baskets, tins, bags, Christmas ornaments, buckets, broken machinery, sculptures, toys... It went on and on. Most of it was old, and most of it was junk – as though Mrs Salamanca had raided every skip in Brooklyn. About the only thing that there wasn't was *furniture*. Not a stick – just big cushions on the floor. Unless you counted a wooden cable wheel (which I didn't), there wasn't even a proper coffee table. Although it seemed unlikely given the curtains of cobwebs that hung in every corner, I could only assume that Mrs Salamanca had sent the sitting-room suite out to be cleaned.

"It's amazing," I finally managed to say. "I've never seen anything like it before." Which was also definitely true. "Where will you put the sofa and the rest of the furniture when they come back?"

"Come back?" She blinked. "Come back from where?"

The survivors of the *Titanic* had nothing on me. I clung on to my smile like a drowning woman to a tea tray. "From being cleaned?"

Mrs Salamanca did her last-gasp-of-the-crane impersonation again. "Oh, it's not being cleaned. We don't have any furniture. I don't really feel it's necessary, do you?"

Of course not. Why clutter up the house with chairs and tables, et cetera, when you could use the space for old biscuit tins and papier mâché fish?

Fortunately I was saved from having to comment on this extraordinary statement by Gallup and Tampa. Tampa was demanding that we go to the park.

"Please," she whined. "We can show Soap the lake and stuff."

I said, "Actually, my name's—"

Gallup pulled my arm – the one that wasn't still rubbing my head. "You want to see my pig?"

"Your pig?" I nearly laughed with relief. As the proud owner of over seventy-five stuffed animals I felt that I'd finally found something I could relate

**40**

to. "I'd love to see your pig. I have three little pigs at home myself." Gallup ran off but I kept on talking. "And thirteen bears and an anteater. But the only animal I brought with me is Bunny." Just the thought of Bunny made me want to cry. For all I knew, he was halfway to Chicago by now.

I was still thinking about Bunny when Gallup returned and thrust something in my face. "This is Bart."

Bart grunted and something that could have been pig drool dripped onto my chin. I screamed. Undeterred, Bart started to eat my hair.

"For God's sake, Gallup!" Mrs Salamanca hauled him off me. "Give Soph a break, will you? She just got here."

"Sophie. And it's fine." Looking out for more hanging fish, I put a few more inches between me and Bart. "I'm sorry I screamed like that. I didn't know he meant a real pig."

Mrs Salamanca suggested that I might want to rest while she did something about supper. She put an arm round me and turned me towards the stairs. "Tampa will show you where Cherokee sleeps."

"Cherokee?"

"Cherokee." Mrs Salamanca gave me a smile that was almost as puzzled as mine. "You know, my other daughter?"

Since Mummy'd told me that her daughter's name was Cherry, I hadn't even heard Mrs Salamanca say Cherokee when she mentioned her before.

**41**

"Oh." I laughed. "Oh, Cherokee." Cherokee – like the Indian. I felt like asking if that meant she'd been conceived on a reservation.

"Dig out some of Cherokee's clothes for Soph until her bag shows up," Mrs Salamanca shouted after Tampa as she thundered down the hall. "And *shoes*!"

I kept smiling so she wouldn't know how much this suggestion horrified me. "Oh, no, that's all right. I don't want to be any trouble."

"Don't be silly." Mrs Salamanca gave me a shove towards the stairs. "It's no big deal. You can't stay in that dress. You want to make yourself comfortable. And you have to get out of those heels. You're limping."

I doubted I'd be comfortable for the rest of the summer – which made limping the least of my problems.

"Well, if you're sure..."

Upstairs seemed even more packed than the ground floor. Among the several things attached to the ceiling was a radiator. I walked under it quickly in case it chose that moment to fall down.

Tampa was waiting by a glossy black door. She gave it a kick and it swung open. "This is our room, Soap!" she announced.

"Sophie." I forced myself to look pleased. "Oh, how nice," I said. "We get to share."

I'd rather have lived on the street.

Tampa's side of the room was painted bright orange, which coordinated well with Cherokee's

42

side – which was black. At least, what I could see of it was black. She was obviously her mother's child, because every available millimetre of space was covered with pictures, skulls, crosses, old bottles with candles stuck in them, and gargoyles. Not only was there a very realistic bat dangling from the ceiling, but what looked to me like a very real bird's claw holding several mangy-looking feathers as well.

"Precisely who is your sister?" I asked. "Morticia Addams?"

"No, stupid," said Tampa. "Her name's Cherokee."

I didn't explain that I'd been joking, because I suddenly realized that there was something missing. "Where's the bed?"

"That's it." Tampa pointed to what I could now see wasn't just a pile of clothes and shoes and books and bags and God knows what on the floor, but a pile of clothes and shoes and books and bags and God knows what on top of a mattress on the floor.

Talk about living on the street.

"Oh," I said. "How Japanese."

"It's a mattress," said Tampa. "And that's her drawers."

"Her drawers?" I eyed the mattress warily but about the only thing I didn't see was a pair of knickers.

"Yeah, here." Tampa kicked the black filing cabinet next to the mattress. "Everything on the bed is dirty but the stuff in here's clean. You can help yourself."

"Thanks. That's really brilliant." There's nothing like a mattress full of dirty clothes to make a person feel at home.

After Tampa left I felt myself drawn to the window like a moth to a flame. Below me stretched the garden of the Salamancas. It was nothing like Mummy's (which has been photographed for a magazine article). About the only good thing that could be said about the Salamancas' garden was it was small.

Instead of my old Wendy house, which Mummy uses as a studio, there was a shed made out of old doors and bits of wood. Instead of a pond there was a dragon made from old tins. Instead of the neat and weeded banks and borders and prize-winning roses there was a jungle of plants whose seeds had probably been blown there by the wind.

And there was no view of the Empire State Building either. Not unless they'd shrunk it and hung plants in the windows.

I was *traumatized*. *Traumatized* as in what had ever possessed me to leave my lovely home and normal parents to live with the Salamancas? It was no wonder Cherokee had jumped at the chance to trade places – I should've thought she would have been happy to trade with anyone who wasn't in prison.

I stood there for a few minutes, too stunned to move. I was tired, I was hungry, I was jet-lagged

– and suddenly I felt about a million miles from home.

I turned back to the room and made a space for myself on the mattress. And then I sat down and cried.

# Things Are Bad –
# Then Things Get Worse

Even though she never does it herself, Mummy always says to look on the bright side of things. So after my crying fit that's what I decided to do.

After all, it wasn't as if I was going to be stuck in Brooklyn for the rest of my life – it was only a few weeks. And it could have been worse – I could have been stuck in Texas or somewhere like that. At least in Brooklyn I wasn't hundreds of miles and thousands of cows away from civilization. Mrs Salamanca said New York was only twenty minutes away on the tube. Easy-peasy.

There was no lock on the door of our room, so I took a clean T-shirt and jeans from the filing cabinet. I opened the wardrobe, looking for shoes, and was nearly suffocated by a landslide of clothes that had apparently been shoved in rather than hung up. Once I'd cleared the debris I found a pair of black high tops with holes in the toes. I limped into the bathroom to change.

The bathroom was smaller than the downstairs loo at home and I stepped into the cat litter tray not once but *twice* getting dressed. Bright side ... bright side ... I said to myself, for heaven's sake, think of the bright side... The bright side was that Pancho Villa didn't only poo in the hall. I could only hope it was possible to brush one's teeth while holding one's nose.

When I had finished dressing and pouring antiseptic lotion over my feet I washed my face and hands, and then I stood in front of the bathroom mirror. The T-shirt was black with red lettering that said IF WAR SOLVED ANYTHING WE WOULDN'T ALWAYS HAVE TO HAVE ANOTHER ONE, and the trainers made me look shorter because I was used to wearing heels. I looked like one of those composite photographs – like when they take the head of Mrs Thatcher and put it on the body of a cancan dancer or a kangaroo.

I raised my chin and stared at the unsmiling stranger gazing back at me. You've only just got here, I told myself. You're just not used to it. Things can only get better.

Comforted, I threw myself a victory sign and went downstairs to ring Mummy, who by now would be worried sick that something had happened to me.

Mrs Salamanca was in the kitchen doing something about supper. The kitchen table was *absolutely* buried under piles of post, papers, material, magazines, books, toys, et cetera. God knows how we were meant to eat dinner. Mrs

Salamanca was at the worktop, chopping vegetables and cubes of cheese.

At the sight of food my stomach growled and
my spirits rose. "Oh, I love cheese," I said. "What
are you making?"

"Brown rice, steamed vegetables and tofu,"
answered Mrs Salamanca.

I could feel my spirits take a little dip, but I
managed to smile back. "Oh," I said, "tofu." It
looked like cheese to me. "I've only had it once
before." When Mummy and Daddy took me to
a Chinese restaurant and I ordered it by mistake.
It was like eating sponge.

"Oh God…" Mrs Salamanca slapped her forehead. "Don't tell me I forgot to tell Carrie that
we're vegetarians."

It took me a second to realize that "Carrie" was
Mummy. Everyone else calls her Caroline. I said
that apparently she had. I said that it was fine, really,
because since the mad cow scandal and the foot and
mouth crisis Mummy pretty much stayed away
from red meat, although British beef was more or
less all right now so we did have the occasional
steak. "And Daddy does love a leg of lamb," I
added. "He says sheep were put on this earth to
be roasted with garlic and thyme."

"Don't let Gallup hear you say that," Mrs
Salamanca advised me. "He's very passionate about
animal rights."

I laughed. The only thing I'd been passionate
about when I was nine was my silver trainers. I said

**48**

I'd be careful. Then I asked if I could ring Mummy. I put my address book on the worktop and explained that I had a charge card number so it wouldn't be on her bill.

"Of course you can," said Mrs Salamanca. "*Mi casa es tu casa* – make yourself at home."

I'd sooner have made myself at home in the doorway of Marks & Spencer.

The second I picked up the receiver Gallup and Tampa appeared in the kitchen as though summoned. Gallup was trying to separate Bart from a small lamp. Bart had the cord in his mouth and wasn't about to let go.

"You two keep quiet," ordered Mrs Salamanca. "Soph's calling England."

"I want to talk to Harry Potter," clamoured Tampa. "And Harriet."

Mrs Salamanca sighed. "Not now," she hissed. "Shut up for a few minutes."

As soon as I heard Mummy's voice I was overcome with the desire to tell her the truth – that I'd swapped my lovely bedroom with en suite bathroom in a large, attractive house, in a desirable residential neighbourhood among normal people, for a mattress on the floor in a shared room, in a cramped, decrepit, unfurnished shack in a grey road with a broken pavement – and beg her to let me come home. But I couldn't.

For the first (and just about *only*) time during my visit, Tampa and Gallup did what they were told. They shut up. Planted either side of me, they

**49**

were as quiet as mice. Even Bart looked mes-
merized.

Once Mummy knew that I hadn't got off at the
wrong stop or been gunned down while I was
crossing the street, she launched into a long account
of how "Cherry" was settling in and what they
were going to do with her in the next few days.

I listened politely. "That's brilliant," I said.

And, "Really? I'm sure she'll love that."

And, "Oh, I'm so glad."

While Mummy banged on about a ride in the
country and a pub lunch and getting tickets for
*Les Misérables*, Pancho Villa squeezed through the
cat flap. I'd always thought cats were attractive animals, but Pancho Villa killed that concept stone
dead. He was all black, was missing part of one ear
and was bigger than a small dog. He glared at me
from across the kitchen.

When Mummy finally came up for air I tried to
give her some hints as to what was really going on
across the pond.

"Oh, and guess what?" I said. "Gallup has a pet
pig!"

"Isn't that nice," said Mummy.

"And you know what else? I get to share a room
with Tampa – she's seven, you know."

"Isn't that nice," said Mummy.

"And you know what the best part is?" I smiled
grimly into the receiver. "You forgot to tell me,
but they don't even live in New York proper; they
live in Brooklyn – which makes my holiday truly

unique. Only the Beckhams have ever been to Brooklyn."

"Well, that really is something, isn't it?"

I glanced from Tampa and Gallup (who looked like they were trying to memorize every word I said) to Mrs Salamanca (who was throwing the uncooked tofu on top of a bowl of rice with gay abandon) to Pancho Villa (who was about to do something unspeakable on the kitchen floor) to Bart (who had let go of the lamp and was scuttling out of the door).

"Yes," I said, "it really is excellent."

How lucky could one person be?

# My Ancestors Didn't Survive the Plague, the Peasants' Revolt and the Civil War by Giving Up

Although Brooklyn and the Salamancas weren't *at all* what I was expecting, my nature is not only resilient, it's also optimistic. That's what having a strong sense of history and tradition does for you. I reckoned I'd feel a lot better after I got some rest. Nana Bea says *everything* looks better after a good night's sleep.

But despite the fact that I was physically exhausted, emotionally shattered and half starved (tofu, like larvae, is only food if you have nothing else to eat), I could only have slept less if I'd been on a sinking ship full of mosquitoes that were devouring me alive.

I lay awake sweating silently in the dark. The Salamancas were obviously the only people in America who had never heard of air conditioning – which meant that I needn't have bothered packing the two jumpers and the jacket, though if I didn't get my bag back I needn't have bothered packing anything. Part of me (the dull, passive part created by Mummy) wanted to tiptoe out of the house, hail a taxi and go straight to the airport. But besides the fact that I had promised Mummy I wouldn't go out alone at night, I couldn't forget that through my veins coursed the blood of Henry II. My ancestors had survived the Black Death, the Peasants' Revolt and the Civil War, and (as Nana Bea likes to say) put the Great in Britain. I owed it to them to at least give the Salamancas a chance. If my ancestors could survive all they survived, then surely I could survive Brooklyn (even with Mrs Salamanca and her brood in it).

Eventually I adjusted to the desert temperature enough to be lulled into a fitful sleep by the fan that (of course!) whirred over my room-mate's head.

Tampa woke me up.

"What if the planets collide?" she shouted. "What if the planets collide?"

I sat bolt upright the way I did at Nana Bea's cottage that time the bat got in. My heart was pounding so loudly that for a moment I thought someone was drumming outside. I knew where I wasn't – I wasn't at home in my own bed – but I didn't have a clue where I was until I stopped hyperventilating enough to realize that I was lying on the floor and I was sweating.

Dear God, I thought, I'm at the Casa Salamanca. It wasn't all some horrid dream.

"What if the planets collide?" Tampa shouted again. "What if the planets collide?"

"Tampa?" I peered into the darkness, but all I could make out was the shape of her mattress. "Tampa, what's wrong?"

In a completely normal voice Tampa said, "I'm going to hang him by them if he eats my violin strings one more time."

I assumed she meant hang the pig.

"Tampa?" I said a little more loudly. "Tampa, are you all right?"

"But why can't I have more chocolate cake?"

That was when I realized she must be asleep. I wasn't sure what to do. I remembered Mummy saying something about not waking sleepwalkers, but I wasn't certain whether or not that went for sleeptalkers as well. I decided not to take any chances.

I lay back down, closed my eyes, put my hands over my ears and recited the Lord's Prayer over and over until I finally dozed off again. (This is a trick Nana Bea taught me. It's much more soporific than counting sheep and it scores points with God.)

But every time I nodded off Tampa would start shouting about the planets or whining about chocolate cake again. If ever a child needed strong medication this was the one.

Eventually I slept enough to dream. We were in France. Mummy, Daddy and I were sitting on the patio eating caviar canapés. Mummy was saying how glad she was that we'd gone to France after all, when a cockerel started crowing. We all

54

laughed because it wasn't dawn – it was dusk. Daddy said, "That's the French for you; even their chickens do things differently." Then Mummy and Daddy vanished the way people do in dreams, but the cockerel kept crowing. I woke up.

By then I'd woken up so many times that I knew precisely where I was – and I knew I wasn't dreaming any more. But I could still hear the cockerel. It sounded like he was right outside the window.

Good Lord, I thought. It's a real cockerel.

God knows why I was surprised. I'd been there over twelve hours.

The only thing that looked better in the morning was the kitchen table. The night before, we'd eaten cross-legged on the floor of the sitting room balancing our plates on our knees, but now enough space had been cleared so that the Salamancas, including Pancho Villa, were all sitting around it having breakfast.

Mrs Salamanca looked up as I came into the room. "So how'd you sleep, Soph?"

"Sophie," I corrected. "Just fine, thank you. The mattress is really surprisingly comfortable without a box spring." Pancho Villa didn't respond to being shooed so I carefully lifted him from the fourth chair and set him on the ground. "Though I do find the heat a bit much," I added.

If I hoped this was going to get me my own fan I was wrong.

Mrs Salamanca laughed. "If you think this is hot, just wait until August."

Oh, thank God, I thought. Something to look forward to.

"It's the oddest thing…" I said as I brushed the chair with the sheet of kitchen roll that seemed to be my serviette and sat down. "But I could have sworn I heard a cock crowing this morning."

Tampa wanted to know what a cock was.

"Rooster," said Mrs Salamanca.

"That's Houdini," said Gallup through a mouthful of half-chewed cereal. "He lives in the backyard."

"Oh really?" I tried to look as though this was one of the most charming things I'd ever heard. "I didn't realize people kept fowl in Brooklyn."

"Only to torture and kill them," he said.

Apparently Houdini had escaped from some voodoo ceremony in the park (one would think I would have guessed that!) and Gallup found him and brought him home.

"Gosh." I managed a laugh. "In England people have picnics and play ball games in the parks." I made a mental note to stay out of the park – no matter what.

"So what would you like to eat?" asked Mrs Salamanca. "There's muesli or toast or you can fix yourself an egg if you want."

I'd never actually cooked an egg on my own except in the microwave, and although there was a bicycle wheel, an angel made out of coat hangers and a real tree in the kitchen, I didn't see one of those. "I think I'll just have toast."

Mrs Salamanca shoved the toaster towards my side of the table. "You have to watch it; it's manual eject."

I took this to mean that, like the car door and the seat belt, the toaster didn't work.

"You want some coffee?"

"Oh no," I said. "Tea will be fine."

"Damn!" Mrs Salamanca slapped her forehead – a gesture I was already beginning to tire of. "I knew I forgot something. I don't suppose you like camomile?"

I didn't suppose that I did.

"It's fine," I assured her. "Really. I'll just have some juice."

Mrs Salamanca told Gallup to pass me the jug of juice. There were cat hairs floating in it and something that looked like it had once been an oat flake.

"You know what," I said, "I think I'll just have water. Water's very healthy."

Mrs Salamanca sipped her coffee. "I thought we'd take it easy today to give you a chance to recover from the flight. We can hang around the house till your luggage turns up, and then maybe take a tour of the neighbourhood – do a little grocery shopping." She winked at me over her cup. "Get you some proper tea. I've arranged it so I don't have to go to work till Monday, so we have time to settle you in."

57

There was something about the way she said "go to work" that made me think she was planning to leave the house.

"I thought you must have a studio in the garden," I said. "Like Mummy."

Mrs Salamanca treated me to her bird impersonation again. "Oh, I don't make my living as an artist." Without even looking she slapped the toaster I'd forgotten about and released two pieces of smouldering bread – my breakfast. "I have a day job."

Mrs Salamanca's day job was as a shopkeeper.

Mummy is friendly with Mrs Mullawah in the corner shop, but they don't travel in the same social circles. Mummy's friends are all professionals or married to professionals. At least I'd thought they were. I tried not to show my surprise.

"Oh, really? Mummy didn't say."

Mrs Salamanca made a *what can you expect?* sort of face. "That's Carrie, isn't it? She'd forget her head if it wasn't bolted on."

And this from a woman who couldn't even remember how to get to the airport.

I tried to scrape the carbon from my toast as discreetly as I could. "What sort of shop is it?" I asked.

"It's called Hunter Gatherers," offered Tampa.

Unlikely as it seemed, I thought that, perhaps, since they were veggies, it was a health food store. I supposed one could hunt for lettuce. In this house finding anything was a hunt. My address book had already gone missing.

Mrs Salamanca shook her head. "Oh, no, I'm not that connected to food."

She didn't have to tell me that – I was on my second Salamanca meal.

More to keep what seemed a relatively normal conversation going than because I was actually curious, I asked what the nanny's name was.

"Sky," said Tampa.

"It's really Andrea," explained Gallup, "but she changed it when she became a hippy and started living in a tepee."

Good God, I thought, these people just get better and better.

"Back up the van, guys," said Mrs Salamanca. "She doesn't mean Grandma." She smiled in my direction. "If you're asking who's looking after the troops while I'm at the store, her name is Soph."

I didn't even bother to correct her. I was too *shocked*. *Shocked* as in why didn't they just call me Cinderella?

"You mean *me*?"

"Carrie didn't tell you that either?" Mrs Salamanca shook her head at this further sign of Mummy's forgetfulness. "That's part of the deal."

Had Mummy told me? I knew she'd mentioned Gallup and Tampa. And she had said something about giving Jacqueline a hand with them. But I'd been so excited to be escaping Putney that I hadn't really grilled her on the details.

"That's the main reason Cherokee couldn't go to Europe with her school," Mrs Salamanca went on. "Because I need someone to look after the kids while I'm working." She wiped jam off her mouth with the sleeve of her Boy Scout shirt. "But you don't have to worry – I promise you won't be too burdened. All you have to do is take them to day camp in the morning and pick them up in the afternoon. You don't even have to fix them lunch. They get fed there."

"Oh," I said. "Well, that doesn't sound so bad." I smiled. "It'll be fun."

Mrs Salamanca's return smile suggested that it might just possibly be less fun than I thought. "I can't believe Carrie didn't tell you…"

I wasn't going to let someone who got lost going to the airport think that Mummy was as disorganized as she was. "I'm sure she did. I must have forgotten – in all the excitement."

"You don't know what excitement is yet," said Mrs Salamanca. "Just wait till you spend some time with these two."

"I'm sure we'll get along famously." I smiled at Tampa and Gallup. "Won't we?"

"Maybe," said Tampa.

Gallup said, "You know your mummy you're always talking about?"

I said yes, quite well, actually.

"Do you think I could see it some day, Soap? I think it'd be cool to have a mummy but Jake won't let me."

60

"Actually," I told him, "my name's Sophie – not Soap."

"I know," said Gallup. "But I like Soap better."

# Eat Your Heart Out,
# Thomas Cook

The reason I couldn't find my address book was because Bart had eaten it. God knows how he got hold of it – the last time I could remember having it was the first time I rang Mummy. Mrs Salamanca finally found its soggy remains underneath the fresh cat poo in the front hall.

"Maybe we should've called them Nixon and Kissinger instead of Bart and Pancho Villa," said Mrs Salamanca. "They're obviously in cahoots."

So because Bart had eaten my address book and I couldn't reach anyone at the airline who could find even a record of my complaint, we stayed in all that first day waiting for my bag to turn up. Which, of course, it never did. The woman who eventually rang from the airline said it was in San Diego. She said they'd get it to me as soon as possible. Mrs Salamanca rolled her eyes and told me not to hold my breath.

I was a bit taken aback by her cynicism. Mummy

might worry about every little thing, but she has a basically trusting nature. It didn't seem to me that Mrs Salamanca's spirit could be the sort that conquered the West. I politely pointed out that it was a British airline so I had every reason to believe that they knew what they were doing.

"Nobody knows what they're doing," said Mrs Salamanca. "That's one of life's great lessons."

On Saturday the man who rang from the airline said my case had moved on to Singapore.

"That's it," Mrs Salamanca announced. "We're not hanging around here any more. Today we're taking the grand tour." She gave me a wink.

Mummy and Daddy were always taking me and Xar on different tours of London when we were little, because Daddy said that most people never explore the place where they live the way they explore places where they don't live. We did all the usual tourist sights – the Tower, London Bridge, the Roman ruins, the museums, Trafalgar Square, the Palace... We also went on several special walking tours, including Dickens's London, Keats's Hampstead, Ghosts by Gaslight, Highgate Cemetery, Roman London, Medieval London, Pagan London and Pepys's London. Not only was it fascinating, but we all learnt a lot – even Daddy.

Of course, London is one of the oldest and most historically interesting cities in the world, which isn't something you can say about Brooklyn.

To give you an idea of just how lacking it is in tourist hot spots, our first stop was Herkimer Street itself.

"Herkimer Street was once a colonial village," Mrs Salamanca informed me as we left the house.

"But before that there was probably an Algonquian village here," put in Gallup. "There used to be a river."

"Gosh." I tried to look as though I found this fascinating. "I thought the Indians were mainly in the Wild West."

"They were everywhere," said Tampa. "Until we killed them all."

Gallup corrected her. "We didn't kill all of them. We only killed most of them."

"Come on, guys." Mrs Salamanca gestured towards the road. "Let's go say hi to the Scutaris."

The Scutaris lived in the house opposite, the turquoise one with the candy-pink trim. As though this wasn't enough to ensure its place in the guidebooks, there was a statue of the Virgin Mary surrounded by Christmas lights on the tiny front lawn, a dozen windsocks and an American flag hanging from the porch, and a sign in the front window that asked: WHAT CAR WOULD JESUS DRIVE?

The Scutaris were sitting on their porch in deckchairs, all dressed the same in baggy shorts, T-shirts and baseball caps, and all overweight in a rather noticeable, let's-stop-at-McDonald's sort of way. I reckoned they were probably as reluctant to go to the park as I was, because they seemed to be

64

having a picnic. There was a full icebox, a portable grill and a table piled with food. Music blared from the radio that was fastened to the railing with duct tape. Obviously duct tape was to Brooklyn what nails were to the rest of the world.

Good Lord, I thought as my eyes fell on the Scutari offspring, she isn't really dragging me over to meet them, is she? Two days ago it wouldn't have seemed possible, but Americans obviously didn't have the same standards as other people. Mrs Salamanca certainly didn't. The Scutari offspring were two young men who looked like they probably had form. They were the sort of blokes you'd race down a dark alley to avoid. One of them even had a knife scar down his cheek.

Well, she can think again, I told myself as I started down the steps.

Mrs Scutari waved and hollered to Mrs Salamanca, "Is that the English girl?"

"It sure is!" Mrs Salamanca hollered back.

"Bring her over!" ordered Mrs Scutari, though it should have been obvious even to someone wearing a Bruce Springsteen T-shirt that this was precisely what Mrs Salamanca was doing.

Mrs Scutari continued to shout across the road. "It's too bad she missed the Fourth, isn't it? She would've met everybody on the block then."

Mrs Salamanca agreed that it was a shame.

The fourth what? I wondered. I was fairly certain it wasn't a fourth for bridge.

All four Scutaris watched me stumble down the

steps because I'd forgotten about the loose railing, and then proceed to trip over the pavement in front of the house because I'd forgotten about that being uneven as well. I righted myself as quickly (and with as much dignity) as I could and followed the Salamancas across the road.

Mrs Scutari whacked each of her sons on the head with the TV guide she was using as a fan as I reached the porch. "George! Errol! Where's your manners?" she demanded. "This girl's come all the way from England."

"That's George after George Washington and Errol after Errol Flynn," explained Mr Scutari. "You know George Washington?"

"Oh, yes," I said. "Back home we call him the English traitor." Which is what Daddy always says, but Mr Scutari didn't think it was as funny as Daddy does.

"He was the father of our country," said Mr Scutari.

By now George and Errol had heaved themselves to their feet to shake my hand.

"How do you do?" I took one meaty hand and then the next. They were cool from the cans of beer they'd been holding. (And it wasn't even noon yet!)

"Umph," said George.

Errol said, "Yo."

Then I shook Mr and Mrs Scutari's hands.

Mr Scutari said, "How ya doin'? I bet this is nothin' like where you come from."

I said he could say that again.

Mrs Scutari said, "Gosh, honey, I really love your accent. I wish I talked like that."

Not as much as I did.

I was about to look at my watch in a significant way when a shadow loomed in the screen door behind them.

"Oh, there she is!" cried Mrs Salamanca, and she yanked open the door and dragged the shadow into the light.

It was a teenage girl with a baby in her arms. She was skinny and her hair stuck up from her head in dozens of bunches fastened with sparkly pink clips, but the baby was fat and bald. The girl was trying to dig something out of her teeth with the longest and pinkest fingernail I'd ever seen.

"Don't let the baby fool you. Barbee here's only a year or two older than you are," Mrs Salamanca informed me.

I said, "Barbie? Like the doll?"

Mrs Scutari said, "Nah. That's what I put on the birth certificate, but she spells it with two e's." She grinned at me over her can of Budweiser. "Always has to be different, our Barbee."

Barbee said, "Ow! Cut it out, Will," as the baby grabbed one of the bunches of hair. She gave me a *what can you do?* smile. "I wear it up like this to stop him from pulling it, as much as because of the heat," she explained.

Good God, I thought. That's her child.

Barbee glanced at Mrs Salamanca and then smiled at me. "Jake thought maybe we could hang out this summer." She wrenched the baby's fingers from another bunch of hair. "Will and me are always looking for someone to go to the park with."

I would have been speechless with relief – thank God it wasn't the yobs she expected me to befriend – if I hadn't been speechless with *horror*. There was no other word for it. *Horror* as in only over my dead body. Surely even Mrs Salamanca couldn't believe I'd come three thousand miles to spend my summer dodging voodoo practitioners with a gym-slip mum. She couldn't be that mad and still be walking around free.

"Oh," I said. "Oh, that would be brilliant." The baby stuck a finger up Barbee's nose. "If I have time. There's a lot I want to do."

Mr Scutari reached into the icebox that just happened to be next to his chair and pulled out a can of beer. "You want one?" He held it towards *me*.

Mrs Scutari slapped him on the side of the head with the TV guide. "Are you nuts, Jerry? She's English. They don't drink cold beer." She smiled in my direction. "That's right, ain't it? You like your beer warm. How about a can of iced tea?"

I still hadn't had a cup of tea since the plane because Mrs Salamanca had forgotten about it and I didn't like to remind her. I was tempted to say yes.

But Mrs Salamanca wasn't.

"We really can't stay, El," said Mrs Salamanca.

"We're doing the tour." She sighed. "And can you believe it? The airline lost Soph's bag, so we have to go to Fifth Avenue and get her some underwear too."

I had one of those rare moments when one wants to jump for joy and die of shame at the same time. I wanted to jump for joy because Fifth Avenue was one of the places I most wanted to see. On the other hand, I wanted to die because Mrs Salamanca was discussing my knickers in public. Never in *ten million years* would Mummy do a thing like that.

Judging by the Scutaris' reaction, however, a person's underwear was something that was publicly discussed all the time in Brooklyn. Not one of them so much as blinked.

"We'll see you later then," said Mrs Scutari. "You guys have fun."

Even if Brooklyn turned out to be more interesting than a bowl of dishwater – which I had reason to believe it wouldn't – it was too hot to have fun. I hadn't been outside for ten minutes and already I was soaked with sweat.

We trudged up one street and down another. Some looked like Herkimer Street, some looked like they were part of an industrial estate, and some looked like they were part of a bomb-site, but there was also a section of Victorian town houses that almost looked like they could be in London.

"The famous brownstones of Brooklyn," my guide informed me. "And that's the old Woolworth mansion."

Besides the old Woolworth mansion, we saw Gallup and Tampa's school. We saw the tree Gallup fell out of rescuing a cat. We went to the park and saw the spot where Gallup caught Houdini and the lake Tampa jumped in because her brother dared her (though, thankfully, we didn't see anyone making blood sacrifices). We saw the corner where Cherokee was hit by a bicycle and the shop where the Salamancas bought their pet food. We saw the building where Tampa had her violin lessons and the building where Mrs Salamanca went for yoga. We saw the place that made the best bagels and the hospital where Gallup had his arm put in a cast when he fell out of the tree. It seemed like every other shop was a Chinese restaurant or a pizza parlour, or had a neon sign that said NAILS in the window.

"People like to eat and get their nails done," said Mrs Salamanca.

And then we got to Hunter Gatherers.

There were more fairy lights in the window than on Oxford Street at Christmas. Because my brother had come back from his travels in "a mood" I knew that the music playing was Tibetan.

Mrs Salamanca introduced me to her assistant manager, a large, dark-skinned woman wearing very bright, traditional African clothes and enormous gold earrings.

"This is Soph. She's from England."

"Sophie," I said through my smile.

"Soph, this is Melody, my right-hand man."

70

I didn't think I'd heard her right. "Melanie?" I said.

"Melody." She laughed. "My mom wanted us kids to always have a song in our hearts."

Of course she did. "Oh. Melody." One could only wonder what her brothers and sisters were called.

Melody answered the question even though I hadn't asked it. "Harmony and Lyric." She laughed again and her gold tooth winked. "I saw you thinkin'." Melody leant over the counter to hug me, knocking over a basket of garish plastic rings. "Welcome to Brooklyn."

"Thank you," I said. And then (because I couldn't think of anything else to say) I said, "So. This is the shop."

Melody scooped rings from the counter and tossed them back into the basket. "It's great, isn't it?"

I smiled again. Great wasn't the first word that leapt into my mind. *Overflow* was the word that leapt into my mind. Anything Mrs Salamanca couldn't cram into the house she'd crammed in here. The only differences were that the shop had air conditioning and looked as if it was cleaned regularly, some of the things were new, and everything had a price tag.

"Yes," I said. "It's great. I – I've never seen a shop like it before." Which was certainly true.

"So," said Melody. "You havin' a good time?"

I picked up the neon-purple rings with orange

71

stripes that had fallen near my feet. "Oh, yes... Very—"

"This is the first time poor Soph's been out of the house," cut in Mrs Salamanca. "Can you believe it? The airline lost her suitcase."

There was a murmur of sympathy from Melody and several of the customers trawling through the aisles.

I held my breath. Oh, please, I prayed. Don't let her mention my knickers...

"We stayed in all yesterday waiting and they never turned up. The poor thing hasn't even had a cup of tea yet because I forgot to get any in."

"They'll probably deliver her stuff while you're out," said Melody. "You know what these airlines are like."

I started to breathe again.

"So that's where we're off to now," Mrs Salamanca continued. "To get Soph some underwear."

And a bag to put over my head if possible.

We re-entered the sauna that is Brooklyn in the summer and trudged down several more long, grey roads, past palm readers and martial arts shops and cheque-cashing establishments.

"Just one more block," announced Mrs Salamanca.

Of course, I knew what Fifth Avenue looked like from films. It was wide and elegant and filled with fabulously expensive shops and disgustingly elegant women loaded down with carrier bags. And even though there'd been no sign of any of these things so far, I still thought that was what I'd see when we turned the corner.

We got to the end of the street. We turned the corner.

The avenue in front of us was a road jammed with honking traffic and lined with cheap shops. There were sale signs plastered in the windows and racks of clothes chained up in front. There were a few young, scraggly trees (all of which looked dead), and the pavement was crowded with men in T-shirts and baseball caps, and women who looked about as elegant as a building crew.

Good Lord, I thought. See Fifth Avenue and die.

"Is this like England?" asked Tampa.

"Not where I live."

Gallup wanted to go and see the iguana in the window of the pet shop on the street we'd just come down. Personally, I wouldn't have let Arnold Schwarzenegger wander about on his own in that neighbourhood, but Mrs Salamanca seemed oblivious to the obvious danger all around us.

"It's perfectly safe," she said to me. "This is a neighbourhood." To Gallup she said, "Wait for us there. We won't take long. We know what we want."

I held my breath, waiting for her to tell everyone on the street that the airline had lost my bag and I needed knickers.

But instead she said, "And no arguing with Mr Miecwiz about how he treats his animals, Gallup.

I don't want another scene. Keep your little butt outside."

Mrs Salamanca, Tampa and I went into the shop on the next corner, which apparently was the best shop around. It was one large room packed with row after row of tables with everything from notebooks to underwear and bath mats to night-gowns piled on them, and more things hanging from the walls. It looked like Poundstretcher having a fire sale.

I was not buying anything that wasn't wrapped, so I ended up with two very purple bras and a packet of knickers with the days of the week on them.

Mrs Salamanca and I were almost at the till when I heard Tampa say something to the cashiers that made them laugh.

I looked at Mrs Salamanca in surprise. "I didn't know Tampa spoke Spanish."

"She just picked it up. She has a gift for languages."

"And what did she say?"

Mrs Salamanca smiled – almost slyly, I thought.

"She said we're here to buy you some underwear because you came all the way from England without your suitcase."

# The Water Life of Brooklyn

I was so completely exhausted from the trauma of having everyone we met told about my knickers, and crawling up and down the dreary streets of Brooklyn, that on Saturday night I not only slept through Tampa but Houdini as well.

I could hear the Salamancas all milling around downstairs and shouting at each other when I did wake up, but I stayed where I was. I'd always been a very social sort of person, but this was the first teensy bit of privacy I'd had since I arrived and I wanted to savour every second. I even picked my nose.

Eventually the possibility of starvation drove me off my mattress. Mummy jokes that one always feels hungry after a Chinese but, believe me, the same goes double for vegetarian meals. I felt as if I were living on water.

I took advantage of the fact that I could actually get into the bathroom without a half-hour wait to take a quick shower before I got dressed. Then, fortified for another day with the family that made the Osbournes look normal, I went downstairs. When I reached the kitchen door I took a deep breath and put a cheery smile on my face, as my ancestors did when the mob of peasants turned up at the gate with burning torches.

As an example of how resigned I already was to the catastrophe my holiday had become, my smile didn't slip one tiny bit when I walked into the room and discovered that the three Salamancas were all ready to be institutionalized.

Tampa was wearing the papier mâché carp, Gallup was wearing a pirate outfit, and Mrs Salamanca was dressed in a seashell made out of loo paper. They were all shouting at each other, but instead of the enthusiastic gestures that usually accompanied their conversations, Tampa was flapping her gills, Gallup was waving his cardboard cutlass and Mrs Salamanca was shaking her shell.

"Good morning, all." My voice was bright and pleasant – as though I was accustomed to coming down to breakfast to find the kitchen filled with sea life. "What's the occasion?"

Gallup, Tampa and Mrs Salamanca all answered at once.

"Pardon? Did you say Neptune?"

"The parade." Mrs Salamanca smiled encouragingly. "Remember? The Neptune Parade?"

"We told you before," scolded Tampa.

"She's English," said Gallup. "She probably forgot."

"Oh, the Neptune Parade." As if people all over the world look at their calendars in July and let out a cheer because it's the month of the Neptune Parade. "Of course I didn't forget. I just... I – I didn't realize it was today."

"*No importa...*" Mrs Salamanca's grin gave new meaning to that old saying "happy as a clam". "But you better hurry and get into your costume. We don't want to be late."

"Me?" My eyes went from one Salamanca to another. "My costume?"

"We wanted it to be a surprise!" Tampa yelled. "Wait till you see it!"

I was counting the seconds.

"Jake made it specially for you," said Gallup.

How *blessed* could one person be?

Mrs Salamanca handed me a parcel wrapped in newspaper and tied with an old Christmas ribbon that showed signs of having been chewed by a pig. "Here. You can consider it a welcome to the New World present."

The only present I wanted from the New World was to go back to the Old one.

I took the packet gingerly. "Oh, you shouldn't have. You really are too ki—"

"Open it," ordered Mrs Salamanca.

Too kind – far, far too kind.

"Why, it's..." I lifted the costume out of the newspaper. It had at least a dozen fronds covered

77

with bubble wrap and painted vomit yellow.

"It's seaweed," filled in Gallup.

I kept smiling. "So it is."

One could only wonder what sort of person made a complete stranger dress up as seaweed.

Mrs Salamanca put an arm round me. "Do you like it?"

Words failed me. I was *dumbfounded*. *Dumbfounded* as in unable to speak without bursting into tears.

"Put it on!" shrieked Tampa.

Gallup whacked several fronds with his cutlass. "Isn't it cool?"

"Oh, it's – it's... I've never seen anything like it before."

"You always say that," said Gallup.

And probably would for the next six weeks.

I kept smiling at his mother and ignored him. "But I'm afraid I'm not really one for dressing up. Back home—"

Mrs Salamanca shook her shell at me. "Oh, don't be so English. Put on the costume. Trust me. You're going to get a real kick out of this."

Oh my God, I thought. Not only are they planning to go outside like that, but they expect me to go with them...

I had no intention of being seen in public with a fish, a pirate and a clam – especially not dressed as seaweed.

"But really—"

Mrs Salamanca laughed. "After I slaved for hours

78

making that amazing costume, you think I'm going to take no for an answer?"

Mummy would have.

"I'm so sorry – I really do appreciate all the trouble you've gone to – but I'm afraid I won't be able to go with you. I'm still a bit jet-lagged." This was true. "And I'm afraid I feel one of my headaches coming on." This was not true, but since it was a miracle that I hadn't, I didn't think it counted as a lie.

Mrs Salamanca said, "Oh, you get headaches too?"

I didn't quite like her tone. "Mummy says it's hereditary."

"Well, in my family painkillers are hereditary. They're in the medicine chest."

"It's all right," I assured her. "Mummy made sure I have my prescriptions."

"Of course she did." She gave me a little shove. "Now hurry up and get dressed. You'll feel a hundred per cent better once you get out in the fresh air."

As if there was fresh air in Brooklyn, right?

I did as I was told, but I was only pretending to go along with Mrs Salamanca's plans. There was *absolutely* no way I was appearing in public as part of an aquarium. By the time we reached the parade my headache would be so bad that I wouldn't be able to get out of the van. I would make myself some space amid the rubble in the back and sleep until the parade was over. I felt this was such a brilliant idea that I gave my fronds a shake in the mirror before I went downstairs.

We took a bus.

Mrs Salamanca, Tampa and I all had to stand in the aisle because our costumes didn't allow for much bending. It was like being on stage.

I know that if I'd been riding on a London bus dressed as seaweed, people would have noticed – but they wouldn't have made a big fuss about it. That would be rude. They'd glance over – and then they'd glance away. They wouldn't gawp. They wouldn't point. They wouldn't shout out personal comments. And they most definitely wouldn't laugh out loud.

But bus passengers in Brooklyn had obviously never heard of social etiquette. Here at last was the American spirit one hears so much about – the one that levelled the Indian population in such a short time. These people didn't worry about anyone else's feelings or space. They gawped; they pointed; they laughed loudly; they shouted out things like, "Honey, you look good enough to eat!"

While all that was going on, Gallup was trying to pop my bubbles with his pirate's cutlass – much to the demented amusement of the criminal type sitting next to him.

No wonder I went into a state of protective shock. Mrs Salamanca and Tampa kept pointing out what they thought were interesting sights, but I was only aware of all the eyes staring at us. It was the first time since the Salamancas had picked me up at the airport that I was happy I was three thousand miles from home. At least no one knew who I was.

I was weak with relief when we finally got to the parade, if only because we weren't the only ones dressed as seafood any more.

There were thousands of people milling about. Considering the fact that no one's heard of Brooklyn, it certainly seemed well populated today. Besides the thousands milling about, there were hundreds more marching or riding on floats.

"Gosh," I said. "It's bigger than I thought."

"Didn't we tell you it's cool?" demanded Tampa.

"It's a Brooklyn tradition," Gallup informed me.

"Gosh," I said. "And what do we have? The royal family and parliamentary democracy."

Mrs Salamanca put an arm round me and gave me a shake. "Trust me, honey. You're going to have a ball!"

The only parade I'd ever been to was a military parade on Putney Heath. It was marked by dignity, order and precision – three qualities completely lacking from Brooklyn in general and the Neptune Parade in particular.

This was chaos disguised as an aquarium.

Everybody was shouting or singing, and most of them seemed to be drinking as well. Any time someone recognized someone they knew they'd call out, "Yo! Over here!" And no one marched in any sort of formation, they just all swarmed more or less forward – unless they saw someone they knew on the pavement and decided to go over for a chat. They jumped on and off the floats at will. They bumped into each other. They wandered out of the group they were with so that one suddenly noticed a lobster in among the shoal of angelfish or a hula dancer leaping about in the middle of a group of snails.

Mrs Salamanca and her changelings were beside themselves with excitement. They jumped up and down, waving and shrieking, whenever they saw a costume they really liked. They took it in turns to call my attention to each new visual delight.

"Look!" Tampa yanked on my fronds. "Look at that killer whale!"

Mrs Salamanca elbowed me in the side. "Get a load of the sea anemone, Soph! Isn't that cute?"

Gallup trod on my foot. "Over there! Over there! It's an axolotl!"

I can't say I found their enthusiasm contagious.

One could have fried an egg on the pavement, it was that hot. And it was particularly hot if one happened to be encased in bubble wrap. A few middle-aged women were fanning themselves with advertising flyers, but otherwise no one but me seemed to notice the heat, unless it was to wipe a forehead with the bottom of a T-shirt. It was an ocean of Brooklynites, and the sweating and belching made it smell like one that was seriously polluted. I tried to squeeze myself smaller so than none of the damp bodies around me would actually touch mine.

After a while I suppose I became hypnotized by the spectacle – that or simply numbed. The costumes were all completely outrageous and over the top – and most of the mermaids seemed to be men – but I started to feel that there was something almost endearing about it. Oblivious to the heat and the stink and how ridiculous a person looks dressed as a fish, these people were actually having a good time.

I was thinking to myself – this really is another country ... this is America ... this is what it's like ... I'm really here ... it's like being the first European to see the Aztecs – when a woman with a pushchair containing one very small shark ran over one of my fronds and, despite the crowd that surrounded us, pulled me to the ground. With me went two men dressed as hula dancers, a large dog dressed as a sailor, and a man wearing a Brooklyn baseball cap. The coconut bra of one of the hula dancers hit me on the head and the man in the baseball cap spilt his beer all over me.

Everybody was shouting, "Are you all right? Are you all right?" At least three people tried to help me up at the same time.

"I'm fine. Really. I'm fine," I repeated over and over. I was *mortified*. *Mortified* as in wanting to drop through the pavement.

Though not as mortified as I was on the bus ride

83

home. Presumably because I smelt like a brewery, people actually stepped away from me as if I were a homeless person or something.

Mrs Salamanca said to look on the bright side (the only time she ever said anything that reminded me of Mummy).

I was practically in the stairwell by the door, trying to keep away from everyone.

"And what would that be?" I asked.

Mrs Salamanca winked. "Seaweed's supposed to smell."

I stared out at the grey and grimy row of car dealers and pizzerias.

Good God, I thought. This is going to be an extremely long summer.

# Mummy Lets Me Down

I had planned to retire to my mattress with a headache the minute we got back from the Neptune Parade, but Mrs Salamanca insisted that I do some yoga with her. "You'll see," she said. "Yoga not only makes you more aware of your body, it's a drug-free way of relieving tension."

The yoga did nothing for the tension, but it definitely made me more aware of my body. Bart started snuffling around my bare foot while I was standing like a tree (which means on *one leg*), and I was so afraid he was going to bite me that I fell over and pulled a muscle. After that Mrs Salamanca let me lie down. I planned to stay in my half of the room all night, but Gallup brought Bart in to apologize, and then Tampa and Pancho Villa came up to keep me company. In the end I gave up and went back downstairs.

Even though I felt that I was a bit of a disappointment to all the generations of my forebears who had risen to every challenge life had thrown at them, I decided I couldn't go on. Aside from the fact that I doubted I'd survive it, I was not spending my precious summer on Herkimer Street. It was out of the question. I'd rather be trapped in a lift with Jocelyn and Daniel snogging than spend another day in Brooklyn.

I reckoned that all I had to do was tell Mummy the whole horrid truth and I'd be on the next plane home. It was obvious that she had no idea what life with the Salamancas was like. She remembered the chum of her youth and assumed that her chum would have grown and matured with the passage of time as she had – as all normal people do. At the very least she would assume that Mrs Salamanca had furniture.

Of course, having a private conversation with Mummy so I could tell her what was really going on was a problem. If Mummy rang me, Gallup or Tampa would answer the phone and bellow, "Soap! It's your mom!" – and then stand there watching me as if I were a talking parrot.

If I rang Mummy, the Salamancas would all appear as though they were dogs summoned by a high-pitched whistle, swarming around me shrieking and banging things while I tried to talk.

But tomorrow Mrs Salamanca would be at the shop and Tampa and Gallup would be at day camp. I'd have the house to myself – and the phone. I couldn't wait. I was practically on my way to the airport.

The following morning I woke up the happiest I'd been since the night before I left dear old England. Even Mrs Salamanca noticed.

"You seem to be in a good mood, Soph." She was power dressed for work in baggy patchwork trousers and a T-shirt with a faded picture of an Indian on it and the words FIVE HUNDRED YEARS OF GENOCIDE. The Christmas tree earrings had been replaced by pigs. "I bet you can't wait to start exploring Brooklyn."

Just call me Sir Walter.

I said that I was practically champing at the bit, but felt I should wait till my case was delivered.

Mrs Salamanca gave me a pitying smile. "I wouldn't count on it coming today, honey."

"But yesterday they said they'd located it in Paris."

"That was yesterday. It's lucky Cherokee's got stuff you can wear. Your luggage is pretty determined to do a world tour."

And oh how I wished I was doing a world tour with it.

"Yes," I said. "I'm very lucky."


Barbee and her baby were already sitting on the Scutari porch watching the air settle over Herkimer Street when Gallup, Tampa and I left the Casa Salamanca that morning.

Barbee waved.

Gallup and Tampa both shouted "Yo!" – which was obviously the greeting used in Brooklyn instead of good morning – but I had my eyes on that tricky bit of pavement in front of the house and didn't see her to wave back.

"Barbee was waving to you," Tampa informed me as I led them up the road.

"Oh, was she?"

"Yeah," said Gallup.

The two of them stared at me as if they suspected I had a bacon sandwich in my pocket. I looked both ways as we came to the corner.

"Barbee's nice," said Tampa.

"And who said that she wasn't?"

"She plays the banjo," added Gallup.

What greater character reference did you need than that?

I decided to change the subject. "You know the other day when Mrs Scutari said it was too bad I missed the fourth?"

"Yeah."

"Yeah."

"Well, what did she mean? The fourth what?"

Gallup thought this was incredibly funny, but Tampa looked shocked. "You mean you don't have the Fourth of July in England?"

"Only as the day between the third and the fifth."

Tampa frowned. "Do you guys have Christmas?"

"Of course we have Christmas. We're a very Christian country."

"What about all the Hindus and Muslims?" asked Gallup.

One could only stare at him in amazement. God knows where he got this stuff from. It was as though he'd lived before and his body was nine but his soul was at least five hundred and ten. "What Hindus and Muslims?"

"The ones who live in England. You know, because you guys took over their countries and exploited them for years, and now it's payback time." Gallup jumped over a line of ants. "I thought there were millions of them."

"Well, there are millions of Christians too," I assured him. "And they all celebrate Christmas."

Tampa explained about the Fourth of July.

"Nobody has to go to work or anything, and they all put flags up and then they all have a picnic or a barbecue or go to the beach, stuff like that, and then at night there's a lot of fireworks. Jake took us down to the river to watch this year."

It didn't sound very special to me. There were always flags up – and if the Scutaris were anything to go by, everyone was always having picnics and barbecues too.

"That's just what we do, dumbo." Gallup gave her a brotherly punch. "It's not what it is."

This time Gallup explained about the Fourth of July. "It's Independence Day." He eyed me coolly. "You know, when we got our independence from you guys. You know, because you had a king and unfair taxation and regular people didn't have any rights."

As if I needed a lesson in the history of my own country from a child. I was beginning to understand why Mrs Salamanca sighed so much – I was beginning to do it myself. "Well, now I know."

The day camp was only a few streets away, but it took us ages to get there because Gallup had to stop and say hello to every cat and dog he saw. I kept a wary eye out for psychopaths and drive-by shooters all the way to the camp. I didn't see any. Almost everyone we passed looked perfectly normal and respectable – business people, and women with children, and workmen. The only dodgy-looking character I saw was a boy around my age walking with his dog on the other side of the road. He didn't look like a psychopath, but he did look like one of those hard-core anarchists the prime minister's always warning us about. You know, with the dreadlocks and the nose-ring and the fifth-hand clothes – the sort you always see up a tree or picketing McDonald's. I changed my mind about crossing at that corner. Before he could notice us – or Gallup could notice his dog – I hurried my charges up the road.

I suppose it's from watching American films, but I was expecting the camp to be outside. You know, with trees and a lake and a tennis court and things like that. Not in the country, obviously, but at least near a chunk of the great outdoors. It was in a church, and the only thing it was near was other buildings.

The woman in charge wore shorts, trainers,

a baseball cap and a tag that said her name was Dawne.

"Pardon me," I said hopefully. "But is this where we come for the day camp?"

It was as though I'd just told her that she'd won the lottery.

"*Oh my God!*" She gave me a hug. "You must be the English girl." She waved to another woman also in shorts and a baseball cap on the other side of the room. "Yo! Lissa! This is the English girl."

Apparently everyone had been told I'd be looking after Tampa and Gallup except me.

Dawne gave me another hug. "So?" She widened her eyes. "Whaddaya think of Brooklyn?"

"Oh." I could only hope I was smiling. "Oh, it's fine. Brilliant – it's really—"

"Brilliant!" shrieked Dawne. "Lissa, did you hear that? The English say brilliant instead of terrific!"

"—different," I finished. "Very different." I meant different to any form of civilization I'd ever known, but Dawne took it as a compliment.

"It sure is, isn't it?" She shook her head – apparently in disbelief. "England! Can you beat that? You came all the way from England. I've never even been to Canada."

It was as though she'd never heard about the invention of the aeroplane, but I decided that I wasn't going to be the one to break the news to her.

"I brought Gallup and Tampa." I gestured to

**91**

where Gallup and Tampa were standing at the side of the room, glowering as though they were Satan's spawn dragged to a Christmas party and expected to play charades. "I don't know if there's anything more I should do. Is there something I'm meant to sign?"

Dawne beamed at me as though I were a chocolate cake. "I *love* your accent. I just love it *so* much. Say that again, would ya, honey? Just one more time."

"Say what?"

"That stuff about if there's more you should do."

I was certain I was smiling now because the muscles of my face hurt. "I don't know if there's anything more I should do."

Two mothers with normal-looking children in tow had come up beside us. The mother wearing bedroom slippers said, "Hey, where are you from? Are you from England? My granddad was in England during the war. He said they didn't even have oranges."

I said we had them now.

"London," said Dawne. "London, England."

The woman in the bedroom slippers said I had a great accent.

I felt like pointing out that if the Americans hadn't revolted she'd have one of her own.


As soon as I got back to the house I went straight to the phone.

It was dead.

My first thought was that Mrs Salamanca hadn't paid the bill. I already knew from some casual remarks made by Gallup that this was something that happened quite frequently. But then I noticed that the cord was just hanging in the air with fingers of different-coloured wires where there should have been a plug. Bart must have got the munchies.

The safe place where I'd written the charge card number had been eaten, of course, but I still had the card itself. I got it out of my purse and went to find a call box.

It wasn't until I was dialling that I noticed the boy I'd seen earlier sitting on a porch across the road with his dog. He made me think of that bloke in *Oliver Twist* – the one who kills his girlfriend. He has a dog too. I turned my back so I couldn't see them.

The way things were going, I wouldn't have been surprised if Mummy hadn't been home, but she answered straight away.

"Eight-seven-nine-eight-double-one-two-seven."

"Mummy?"

It wasn't a good connection.

Mummy said, "Yes?"

Surely she hadn't forgotten me already. "Mummy, it's me." I raised my voice. "Sophie."

"Oh, darling." Mummy laughed. "I *am* sorry. Things are a bit hectic here. You know, with the

93

rain and all." She lowered her voice. "Nana Bea is driving me mad."

"Well then, I've got some good news for you." I grinned at the instruction panel on the phone. "Guess what, Mummy? I've decided to come home early – so I'll be able to give you a hand with everything."

Nana Bea could drive Jesus mad just making a cup of tea, so I reckoned Mummy would greet my announcement with free-range joy – or at least a polite "Why, isn't that lovely, dear…"

"What do you mean, early?" asked Mummy. She didn't sound particularly joyous.

"I mean early – like as soon as you can change my ticket."

Mummy was silent for several seconds while more than one voice shouted behind her, and then she wanted to know what had happened.

"I thought you were having a good time." She said it as though I'd broken some promise.

"I had to say that. They watch me like I'm a rabbit and they're a bunch of hungry hawks. And if you think there's any privacy here, you're wrong. The only time I'm alone is when I'm in the loo."

"Oh, darling—" Mummy began.

I didn't let her continue. I told her about the tofu, the changeling children, the shared room and the mattress on the floor, the cockerel, the pig and the incontinent cat, and the costumes and the Neptune Parade – *everything* – until I could say no more because I was out of breath and close to tears.

94

"And I *still* don't have my things. I have to wear Cherokee's clothes and they're *very* peculiar. I think she may be a lesbian. I haven't seen a single dress or skirt." I was definitely ready to cry.

"But you can't possibly come home. What's Cherry meant to do?"

She was *oblivious* – there was no other word for it. *Oblivious* as in didn't even know the name of her own house guest. Had she always been like that?

"Her name's not Cherry," I snapped. "It's Cherokee." I wiped away some tears. "And she can come back here." It was her home, after all.

"And what if she doesn't want to?" asked Mummy.

"Well then, she can stay in Putney if she's going to be difficult. She can have the spare room."

"We don't have a spare room now that Xar's back," she reminded me. "That was a temporary luxury, remember?"

"But there must be some way… I know – she can sleep on the sofa, or in Daddy's study."

Mummy said no. "Cherry's our guest."

"Cherokee," I corrected. "And I'm the Salamancas' guest, and look how they treat me!"

Mummy said I was being ridiculous. "You've only been there a few days. You have to give it a chance."

Like you have to eat the *entire* apple before you work out that it's riddled with worms, right?

"But I didn't know I was meant to be the nanny. You could have warned me, you know. You could have said that if I came here I'd have to sleep on the floor and be a servant."

Mummy sighed. "I told you there were two young children and Jacqueline needed help with them," she said. "And you're not a servant. All you have to do is take them to their camp or whatever. You'd be walking the dogs if you were at home. I don't see that there's much difference."

"Well there is. Raleigh and Drake both excelled in obedience school."

I'd never realized before how unenthusiastic Mummy's laugh is. "I'm sorry, darling, but I'm afraid it's out of the question."

"But it's so hot. I sweat when I'm standing still. And they don't even have a decent fan."

"Then why don't you buy one?" Mummy suggested. "You have my credit card. You can give it to Jacqueline as a thank-you gift."

Which begged the question of what I was meant to be thanking her for. Letting me sleep on the floor?

"There's nowhere to buy a fan around here."

"Don't be ridiculous," she said. "They must have shops."

The thought of going into one of the dingy shops around Herkimer Street nearly made me sob out loud.

"But, Mummy—"

"I'm sorry, Sophie, I really am." She sighed again. "But I'm afraid I can't turn everyone else's plans upside down because someone spilt a little beer on you. This is what you wanted. You've made your bed, and now you'll have to sleep in it."

"But it isn't a bed. It's a mat—"

"Oh dear," cut in Mummy. "I am sorry, darling, but I'm afraid I have to go. Nana Bea has an appointment with the doctor."

"But, Mummy, I'm lonely." It was nearly a sob. "I don't have any friends." I'd always had friends before – tons of them.

"Then perhaps you should try to make some."

But the friends I'd always had were just like *me*. How could I make friends in Brooklyn? Had she lost her mind? I'd sooner make friends with the Jedi.

"Jacqueline says there's a very nice girl across the road."

Jacqueline seemed to be talking to Mummy more than I was.

"You don't mean Barbee, do you? Barbee Scutari? Oh, Mummy, you can't mean Barbee Scutari. The only thing Barbee and I have in common is some primordial swamp ancestor. I mean, really, Barbee Scutari's a gymslip mum."

"Really?" Mummy didn't sound as shocked as she had when we watched that programme on teenage sex on the telly. "I didn't think they went in for that sort of thing in America. The president doesn't approve."

"Well, apparently he didn't tell Barbee that."

"Of course, I'm sure he doesn't approve of

**97**

drinking or drugs any more either – now that he's given them up."

"Mummy—"

Either it was thundering in Putney or Nana Bea was getting restless.

"I really must go. We'll talk later." And she hung up.

I stood there with the receiver in my hand, staring at it blindly. I now knew precisely how poor Alice felt when she fell down that rabbit hole. The only word for it was *abandoned*. *Abandoned* as in deserted by everybody and everything one had ever relied on.

Wait till you get in the house to cry, I told myself. You don't want to make a public spectacle of yourself.

It was a few minutes before I realized that I was already making a public spectacle of myself. Through a blur of tears I saw the boy and the dog on the porch across the road stand up. The two of them started down the steps. At least one of them was looking right at me.

Good God, that's all I need, I thought. *English tourist mugged in call box. Witnesses loved her accent.* I slammed the receiver back in place and started walking towards my home away from home.

"Oi! Wait up!"

I couldn't believe it. *Me?* Was he talking to *me?* I risked a quick glance over my shoulder. He and his mutt were on my trail.

My heart rate and pace picked up.

Too late, of course, I realized that this was what happened when one didn't do what one was meant to do. When one wasn't dull and passive but bold and adventurous. One ended up in Brooklyn being pursued by social misfits and their dogs.

I was certain I could hear the dog panting and straining at his leash. He was probably drooling with excitement. Fee, fie, foe, fum... He smelt the blood of an Englishman! Well, of an English girl.

I started to walk even faster. When I got to Herkimer Street I risked another glance over my shoulder. It was a miracle. The boy and the dog were still a street away. God had intervened – the dog was sniffing at a tree. The Casa Salamanca beckoned. Less than an hour ago I wouldn't have thought it possible, but I'd never been so glad to see anything in my life. I ran the rest of the way, tripped over the pavement, hurled myself up the steps and let myself in.

I locked the door behind me and just stood there. I was drenched with sweat and out of breath, but I was safe. There was that to be thankful for. I was indoors and safe.

And then the doorbell rang.

I nearly screamed out loud.

It couldn't be. How could he know which house I'd gone into?

"Oi!" The doorbell rang again. "Are you in there?"

As if I would tell him, right? "Oh, yes, I'm in here, exhausted, defenceless and terrified out of my mind. Shall I open the door so you can mug me and your dog can rip me apart?"

I held myself so rigid I even stopped sweating.

"Oi! It's me! Bobby!"

Well, why hadn't he said so before? It was him! Bobby! That was all right, then. Obviously I was bound to know someone named Bobby.

Either everyone in Brooklyn was completely out of his or her mind or this bloke watched too many cheesy horror films. You know, the sort where the girl is all alone in the house and she knows there's a psychopath on the loose, but when the bell rings she opens the door – and lo and behold, there's a chap in a hockey mask swinging a samurai sword.

Once I was sure he was gone I went into the kitchen. The sink was full of dishes, but I found a chipped Garfield mug and the last clean plate in the cupboard. All I'd had for breakfast was half a slice of burnt toast and the worst cup of tea I'd ever had – one whose only relationship to that noble drink was that the label said it was tea. Other than that it might have been coloured water.

I looked in the fridge, hoping for an unopened carton of juice and anything that wasn't tofu.

Our fridge at home is always full. Mummy sees to that. The freezer is packed with microwaveable meals; the vegetable compartment is stuffed with vegetables; the shelves are stocked with eggs and cheeses and yogurts, et cetera.

Mrs Salamanca didn't see to anything. There was one empty ice-cube tray in the freezer; two carrots and a couple of sprouting potatoes in the vegetable compartment; and juice that someone had been drinking out of the carton, a packet of vegetarian chicken slices that expired three days ago, some cheese slices that looked rather plastic and one egg on the shelves.

I took out one of the carrots. It could bend in half without snapping.

I closed my eyes, thinking of the bright side. It wasn't all that bright (a torch would have helped to be able to see it), but it was better than nothing.

The bright side was that I was only here for the summer.

If I lived that long.

# Shop and Then Drop

Mrs Salamanca brought home some things for breakfast, but she'd had too stressful a day to do any real shopping.

She seemed surprised to discover that there wasn't more in the fridge. She stared into it as though it might tell her where all the food was hidden. She sighed. "Well, there's half a leftover pizza in the freezer. That's something."

Though not a lot if you asked me.

She opened the cupboard. There wasn't much more in there. "Looks like it's tomato soup and pizza," she said.

The only time I ever had soup for supper was when I was ill or we'd had a big lunch – and the soup never came from a tin.

Mrs Salamanca put the pizza in the oven, Gallup heated the soup, Tampa got out the condiments (tomato sauce – she and Gallup put catsup, as they called it, on everything) and I laid the table (it was the only way I could be sure there weren't any cat hairs on the plates).

"So the shop must have been busy today," I said conversationally as we sat down to eat.

"No." Mrs Salamanca smiled sourly as she doled out the soup. "The Big El was busy."

I knew the Big El was the landlord because they talked about him the way Mummy and Daddy talked about the weather – as a constant source of unhappiness.

"What's that mean?" asked Gallup.

Mrs Salamanca had a wide range of sighs. Her Big El sigh was full of suffering. "The lease is coming up on the house and the store so he's busting my chops."

Tampa twirled a strand of cheese around her tongue. "Does he own everything in Brooklyn?"

"He might as well," said Mrs Salamanca. "He owns everything connected to us." She wiped some sauce from her mouth with the back of her hand. "The Big El's living proof that you don't get to own half the neighbourhood because you're a nice guy."

I don't like to get involved in other people's personal problems, of course. Trying to look sympathetic, I cut a bit from my pizza and said nothing.

"Doesn't Grandpa Gene know somebody in the Mafia?" Saucy strings of cheese dripped from Gallup's mouth like bloody fangs. "Maybe he could help."

**103**

I knew there was always room for improvement, but obviously there was always room for surprise as well. I must have looked a bit more shocked at the news that the Salamancas had Mafia connections than I intended, because Mrs Salamanca immediately said, "Of course he doesn't, Gallup. And anyway, I don't want the Big El dead – I just want him to undergo a spiritual transformation and give us a break."

I picked up my piece of pizza with my fork, trying to think of some way of changing the conversation to something less personal and loaded with doom.

Tampa did it for me. "Soap?"

I looked over. She was holding her slice in the air and staring at me as though I'd just stepped off the mother ship.

"Is that the way you eat pizza in England?" she asked. "With a knife and fork?"

"Of course it is." I didn't want to seem rude, but I was pretty repulsed by all the leaking sauce and cheese. It was like eating with lions. "We always use a knife and fork. Cutlery is one of the great benefits of civilization."

"Second only to gunpowder," said Mrs Salamanca.

"It must be hard eating cereal," said Tampa. "Doesn't the milk fall through?"

So because Mrs Salamanca's landlord would have made Hitler look like a slave to compassion, I was given the job of buying the groceries after I picked up Tampa and Gallup the next afternoon. Mrs Salamanca said they could help me carry the bags, which was fine with me. I had enough trouble carrying myself in the heat. She said it would be an experience. One could only hope it wasn't a *bad* experience, though, to be honest, after a day with nothing to do but watch telly ads (there were so many that I could never remember the actual programmes), I wasn't all that bothered. I was almost looking forward to having something to do.

We went to the supermarket near Fifth Avenue. It wasn't as big or as new or as bright as the superstore Mummy went to, but it did have air conditioning, which immediately made it a big hit with me. I reckoned we might be spending a lot of time in there if the heatwave didn't break.

"We'll need a trolley," I said as I took out the list Mrs Salamanca had given me. Unlike Mummy's shopping lists, which she prints out from the computer, it was written in crayon on the back of an old envelope.

"You what?" asked Tampa.

I repeated the word "trolley".

"You mean like a train?" asked Gallup.

"No, I mean like a basket. To carry the groceries. We forgot to bring the mule."

"Oh, I get it," said Gallup. "She means a shopping cart."

What would I do without him? He was better than a phrase book.

"Why can't you just speak English?" asked Tampa.

Gallup pushed the trolley and Tampa hung off the front impersonating a siren. I pointed out that this would not have been considered appropriate behaviour in London.

"But you're not in London," said Gallup. "You're in Brooklyn."

Which was all too true.

It all went astonishingly well. Although there was almost an entire aisle where everything was labelled in Spanish, and there were three shelves of candles in large jars decorated with pictures of Jesus and his friends, there were also the usual aisles of cereals and snack foods and tinned goods, a deli counter, and a produce section. I wouldn't say I felt at home (at home no one would ask me where I was from every time I spoke), but at least I was somewhere familiar.

This success made me confident. So confident that when Gallup wanted to stop by the pet shop next door to see the iguana, I said, "But not for long. We've got things that will melt."

The iguana was in the window. He was a young tree iguana, small and blue-green. He had a bowl of water, sand and a branch. He looked like he'd been drugged. I reckoned that the only reason he wasn't sweating was because he'd been baked dry.

"Do you think he dreams of home?" asked Gallup. "Do you think he wonders how he ended up in a window on Ninth Street?"

"I bet he misses his mom," said Tampa.

It'd never happened to me before, but I found myself sympathizing with a lizard. At least I knew that my dreams of real tea and a room to myself were going to come true some day. And I was going to see my mum again; she wasn't wandering through the jungle wondering where I'd gone.

I turned my head to rub my eye.

Coming towards us from Fifth Avenue were a boy and a dog. The boy was listening to his Discman and the dog was carrying a bedroom slipper that looked like a bear's head.

Good God, I thought. It's like being haunted.

Even though there were a lot of people about, so I doubted he would try to mug me, I didn't want him to see me. I certainly didn't want Gallup to see the dog and involve us in a conversation.

"Come on," I said, "let's look inside."

Gallup was through the door before I'd finished my sentence, but Tampa looked up at me, frowning. "But I thought Jake said—"

"Did you hear me? Let's go and look at the budgies."

"The what?"

"The birds." Why did these people have to have a different word for everything? "Let's go and look at the birds."

"But Jake—"

"Never mind that." I gave her a gentle shove through the door. "I'm in charge now."

The pet shop was as packed to the rafters as the Casa Salamanca and Hunter Gatherers. There were walls of tanks and cages and several narrow aisles between the shelves full of pet food and accessories. I was beginning to wonder if there was something about Americans that made them dislike uncluttered space. No wonder they had levelled the wilderness to build cities and towns. It must have driven them mad.

"God help us," I said as I followed her inside. "It's just like home."

Always a stickler for accuracy, Tampa said, "No it isn't. We don't have so many animals."

Except for the man behind the counter and the man who was talking to him about baseball, we were the only ones in the shop. I kept watch at the entrance while Tampa checked out the fish. Gallup was already on the other side of the room.

I held my breath as the boy and the dog strolled past the pet shop, but neither of them so much as glanced in. I counted to sixty – slowly – and then I poked my head out of the door. They were just clearing the supermarket. I watched them till they reached the next corner: *coast clear*.

"Gallup! Tampa!" I called. "Let's go before we end up with chocolate-chip soup."

I picked up my bags and opened the door. I was expecting some resistance from Gallup, but he sped past me, his carrier bag clutched to his chest.

"Slow down!" I called after him. "It's too hot to walk so fast."

Gallup, of course, paid no attention to me. He was halfway up the road by the time Tampa joined me at the door.

"He's up to something," she said.

We stepped into the street. "Maybe he has to go to the loo."

"The what?"

"The bathroom."

"Don't count on it," warned Tampa. "I can tell when he's up to something."

Gallup marched on ahead of us all the way home. He was sitting on the front porch when Tampa and I turned into Herkimer Street.

"What's that?" asked Tampa as we trudged down the road.

"It's your brother. Don't tell me you've forgotten him already."

"Not *him*." For a seven-year-old she was pretty good at sounding scornful. "In the bag. I told you he was up to something."

A tiny blue-green head was poking out between a box of cereal and a bag of crisps.

"I don't believe it." I picked up speed. "Gallup Salamanca," I yelled. "What have you done?"

Gallup pushed the tiny head down in the bag and gazed at me innocently.

"Nothing," he said.

"Don't tell me nothing. There's an iguana in that bag."

His expression turned from innocence to defiance. "So?"

**109**

"So that's stealing. You can't go around stealing iguanas."

"I didn't steal him." Gallup lifted the iguana gently from the bag and held him in his arms. "I liberated him." He glared at me.

"You sound like a politician." I glared back. "I don't care what you call it. You *stole* an iguana."

"You saw him! He would've died in that window!" he shouted. "I had to save him."

I'd never been an accessory to a crime before. I'd never so much as nicked a chocolate bar from the corner shop.

"That isn't the point. You can't just go around taking other people's property."

"But he would've *died*!" Gallup was screaming in earnest now. "Is that what you wanted? Iguana blood on your hands? Couldn't you see how unhappy he was?"

The iguana blinked. He certainly didn't look unhappy now.

"What are we going to call him?" asked Tampa.

"Bill," said Gallup.

I sighed. To my surprise, of the two thoughts running through my mind at that moment, neither was about going to jail. The first was that even the Salamancas' had to be better than being imprisoned in a window. And the second was that I hoped he wasn't peeing on our supper.

I took out my key. "All right," I said. "But you're the one who's telling your mother."

# I Don't Buy a Fan

Mrs Salamanca didn't bat an eyelash when she came home to find an iguana in the bathtub. She sighed a few times, and then she picked up the phone and called Mr Miecwiz, the owner of the pet shop. Mr Miecwiz didn't want the iguana back. He said if she'd solemnly promise to keep Gallup out of his shop for the rest of his life he could keep the damn thing. He said it was more trouble than it was worth.

"Like you," Mrs Salamanca told Gallup. "And you'd better make him a safe temporary home until you've got his vivarium set up. Poor Soph doesn't want to spend tomorrow chasing an iguana around the house."

That was the last thing poor Soph wanted to do. Emboldened by my successful trip to the super-market, I'd already decided that after I dropped Gallup and Tampa off the next morning I'd follow Mummy's advice and buy a fan. This might be my summer of hell but that didn't mean I had to experience it literally. And if I was ever going to take that twenty-minute tube ride into the real New York City on my own I needed to build up my confidence – and that was something I had to do. Not only so I stayed sane, but so when I got back home and people asked me what I'd done, I could say more than, "I watched television adverts, rang the airline and helped liberate an iguana." I reckoned that a solo journey in Brooklyn would be good practice.

Of course, I had no idea where to buy a fan. I could have asked Barbee, but I was not going to follow Mummy's advice about making friends – not with Barbee Scutari at any rate. What were we meant to talk about? Nappy rash?

So I asked Dawne.

Dawne knew a great place on Flatbush Avenue. It was the biggest and cheapest appliance store in Brooklyn. Dawne bought everything there. I could get a bus that would take me right to the door.

"Soon as you see the big chicken you pull the cord and get off at the next stop," said Dawne.

It's not as if I'd never been on a bus before. I took buses in London all the time. But the bus I caught following Dawne's instructions was like a London bus only in the sense that it had wheels, passengers and the driver was grumpy.

"Pardon me," I said. "But I'd like to buy a ticket."

Without taking his eyes from the traffic the

driver pointed to the contraption beside him. "Puddit in there."

"Pardon?"

He turned his head and looked at me. Coldly. "In there," he repeated. "Put a buck fifty in there."

I held out a five-dollar bill. "Does it give change?"

He shook his head. "No, honey, it don't give change."

"Well, what do I do? This is all I have."

The driver sighed. "You ain't from around here, are you?"

"No," I answered. "I'm from London."

"In Connecticut?"

I didn't even know where Connecticut was.

"In England."

He continued to gaze at me for a few seconds and then he pulled a lever and the door closed behind me. "Just take a seat, Miss London in England." We edged into the traffic. "Welcome to Brooklyn."

It wasn't until I turned to the rest of the bus that I realized I'd made a mistake.

Almost all the other passengers were black, and the ones who weren't weren't really white. I'm not prejudiced, of course, but I did feel outnumbered. And they all seemed to be looking at *me*. Not as if they were planning to mug me or anything like that – as if they couldn't imagine why I was on this bus either.

Good God, I thought. I'm going to a bad neighbourhood.

I took a seat by the window so I could watch for the chicken. The further we went the better Mrs Salamanca's Fifth Avenue began to look. It was too late now, of course, but I finally realized that the one piece of Mummy's advice I really should have followed was the bit about not going anywhere on my own.

Street after street of fast-food restaurants and bargain stores and small grocers and pawnshops, and off-licences where the entire shop was protected inside with what I assumed was bullet-proof glass, went by.

I began to worry that I had got on the wrong bus. Dawne had said the shop wasn't that far. No more than twenty minutes, even if the traffic was "really crazy". Where was her stupid chicken? I hadn't dared look round before but now I risked a glance. There couldn't have been more than five of us left on the bus, including the driver.

I didn't know what to do. Stay on and end up in one of those urban jungles one's always hearing about? Or get off in the urban jungle I was already in?

I was so tense that when the woman behind me tapped my shoulder I practically jumped out of my seat.

"'Cuse me, honey, but do you know where you're goin'? Do you know where you want to get off?"

I told her where I was going. I could barely hear myself over the pounding of my heart. "I'm meant to get off when I see the chicken."

"You been lookin' out the wrong side of the bus, honey. We passed the chicken ten stops back."

"Oh." I smiled. "Oh, silly me."

She wanted to know where I was from.

"All the way from London. Well, ain't that something. You musta had better directions for that." She got up, took me by the arm and hauled me from my seat. "You get off at the next stop and I'll show you where to go."

Looking neither left nor right, I walked back the way I'd come very briskly, trying to look as though I knew where I was and where I was going.

The shop was exactly where Dawne promised it would be – right across from a large plastic chicken wearing a big smile and a bib. There was only one problem: the shop was closed – because of the fire. Of course.

I was *gobsmacked. Gobsmacked* as in why couldn't it be open – was that *really* so much to ask?

I could feel the sweat dripping down my neck and the backs of my legs, my muscles ached from holding myself so rigid, and my stomach felt hollow from hunger. All I wanted was to be back on Herkimer Street. Right that instant would have suited me fine. I practically ran to the next bus stop.

But the incredible stresses of the morning were beginning to affect me. My mind went blank. I couldn't remember the number of the bus I'd come on. I stared at the route map, but none of the streets marked on it seemed familiar either. And then, of course, there was the matter of change for the fare.

Oh God... Why hadn't I stayed home in Putney? Dull and passive wasn't the worst thing a person could be – the worst thing a person could be was in a coma on a life-support system because of a drive-by shooting.

I could feel the tears welling up inside me. Not only was I stranded in the badlands of Brooklyn, and, as the only completely white person on the street, the perfect target for a senseless, violent crime, but now I was going to cry in public.

I counted to twenty backwards, took as deep a breath as possible even though I could see the air, and started to walk back to the Casa Salamanca, my eyes on the ground, counting the streets so I'd know I was getting closer.

I'd gone five streets when I heard someone shout, "Yo, girlfriend!"

I kept my eyes on the pavement and my feet moving.

"Yo! I'm talking to you."

Much to my horror he was loping beside me. Oh, why did everything have to happen to me?

I didn't even stop at the corner although the light was against me. It didn't stop him.

"Hey, you deaf or something? Where you be going, woman?"

I raised my chin and marched on. He grabbed me by the elbow. I wondered if, before he mugged

me or worse, he'd let me write a note to Mummy
to tell her she'd been right and that I wished I'd
listened to her – just in case I didn't survive the
attack.

I turned to find myself facing a young man who
was wearing a headscarf, a gold crucifix around
his neck, and at least three gold rings. I half
expected him to be holding a flick knife.

"Don't look so scared. I ain't gonna hurt you."
He grinned. "I seen you jetting down the street and
my psychic powers told me that you have got
yourself lost."

I nodded.

"Right. So where is it you're intending to go?"

"Herkimer Street."

"And where's that at?"

I was breathing regularly again. "I'm not certain. I caught the bus up here near somewhere
called the Grand Army Plaza."

"Hey!" He grinned again. "Where you from?"

"London," I said. "London, England."

"That's where the queen lives, right?"

"Her and me," I said.

"You ever see her?"

"Only on telly."

He gave me a look as if I was having him on.
"What's that?"

"Television – TV."

"That what you call it?" He held out his hand.
"My name's Dubois."

I hesitated for a second – I'd never touched a

**117**

man wearing a headscarf before – but then put my hand in his. "I'm Sophie."

"Well, I'm glad to meet you, Sophie." He gave me another big smile. "I sure love the way you talk."

# Every Silver Lining
# Has a Cloud

There was no way I was ever going into Manhattan on my own and that was definite – not after my experience in the wilds of Brooklyn. I reckoned the bus ride alone had taken at least twenty years off my life – I couldn't afford any more. All I had to do was survive a few more weeks and then I'd be home and I could forget all about my nightmare on Herkimer Street. I would put it behind me. When my friends asked me if I'd had a good time, I'd say, "Brilliant." When they asked me how I liked New York, I'd say, "It's the most exciting city in the world." When they asked me what I'd done, and where I'd gone, and what I'd seen, and where I shopped, I'd continue to lie. I reckoned I'd seen enough films to be convincing.

In fact, even though Mr Dubois put me on the right bus, paid my fare and instructed the driver to tell me where to get off, and I did get back in one piece and all, I vowed I wasn't leaving the Casa

Salamanca again unless I *absolutely* had to. So except for taking Gallup and Tampa to and from camp (a long, roundabout route that didn't take us near anyone walking his dog) I was going to dedicate the rest of my summer to watching telly adverts broken up by talk shows and sweating. When I did go out I'd wear Cherokee's vampire sunglasses (they were so dark I walked into things if I wore them in the house) and a baseball cap so even Mummy wouldn't have recognized me.

And that's more or less what I did the rest of that week. I'd take Tampa and Gallup to camp and then I'd go back to the house and ring the airline. That usually took up at least half an hour, most of it spent listening to an instrumental version of "Raindrops Keep Falling on My Head". After the airline had assured me that either they had no idea where my case was or they were certain it was in Tanzania, I'd watch telly and dehydrate until I was so bored I was afraid my brain was dead.

It was more than boring – it was *stultifying*. That's the only word for it. *Stultifying* as in so incredibly boring I would have been willing to watch Jocelyn and Daniel practise mouth-to-mouth resuscitation on each other for days on end. So after a bit I began to deviate from my original plan and, with the help of a book Mrs Salamanca had given me, I taught myself yoga in the afternoons. I reckoned boredom was a form of tension.

\*   \*   \*

Barbee and her baby had been absent from the Scutari porch for a few days, but when I got back to the house the following Monday they were in position on the steps. She was looking right at me as I came round the corner – which meant that I was looking right at her. I had to say hello.

"I thought you'd gone away," I lied.

"Nah." Barbee hefted the baby on her hip and strolled towards me. "We've been sticking close to the AC."

I said I didn't blame her. "It's been hot as blazes. I feel like my bones are starting to melt."

"You should put your hair up. You might as well be wearing a fur hat."

"I was thinking of buying myself a fan."

"Why don't you come over?" she asked. "We could hang out and be cool." She cracked the gum she was chewing. "We've got iced tea."

"Gosh." I tried to look disappointed and keep moving at the same time. "I'd really love to, but I've got a million things to do today."

"Oh, sure." Barbee nodded. "Well, maybe some other time."

"Yeah." I took out my key. "Some other time."

Through the peephole I watched her go back across the road and disappear inside, then I collapsed against the door in relief. Close call... I was going to have to be more careful in future.

I decided that Barbee was probably right about the hair, so I found some butterfly clips in the dragon box on Cherokee's filing cabinet and pulled it off my neck. Then I rang the airline again to see if there was any news (which someone with a negative attitude like Mrs Salamanca could have told me there wouldn't be), and then I settled down in front of the telly with a glass of lemonade.

The telephone rang.

It was Dawne at the day camp.

Dawne said she was really sorry, but she'd given Gallup and Tampa several warnings and there was only so much she could be expected to take and could I please come and take them home.

"Enough is enough," she said.

I said, "Pardon?"

"That's what I love about you English. You're always so polite."

The cold, dank brick of doom was pressing down on my chest. I'd accepted the fact that I was going to have a really rotten summer – the most rotten summer anyone not on drugs could imagine – but now it was getting even worse.

"I'm not being polite, Dawne. I don't understand what you mean."

At least I hoped I didn't.

"Gallup and Tampa." Dawne sighed. "You have to come and get them. I can't have them here any more. They're too disruptive."

"You want me to take them home for the rest of the day?"

"I want you to take them home for the rest of the summer."

"But that's impossible. I – I can't."

**122**

"You have to," said Dawne. "Or I'm bringing them home myself."

What choice did I have? I turned off the telly. I couldn't get the baseball cap on my head with the clips, but I reckoned that my hair up like that was disguise enough, so I put on Cherokee's trainers and dark glasses, and went back the way I'd just come.

Gallup and Tampa were sitting by themselves on one side of the room when I got there. In contrast to their well-dressed camp mates they were both wearing ratty old jeans and trainers. Tampa had declared it a Blue Day when she got up so everything on her was blue, including the dozens of tiny stars clipped in her hair. Gallup had on a T-shirt Jake had made him, which featured a picture of the earth and under it the words LOVE IT OR LEAVE IT. They looked like one of those posters for the government: *Can You Help?* The other children looked like they were in a cereal advertisement (I'd seen so many ads by then I could probably have said which one).

They seemed glad to see me. They both gave me the high sign and rolled their eyes. They seemed to be taking their disgrace a lot better than I was.

Dawne said she thought that Tampa and Gallup were antisocial.

I glanced over at Gallup and Tampa again. It was the first time I'd ever seen them look bored.

"They're not antisocial," I argued. "They're just weird."

123

"That too," said Dawne. "But they exhibit a lot of negative behaviour."

"Like what?"

"They refuse to join in group activities."

"What activities?"

"They wouldn't go swimming when we took them to the pool."

I smiled in a polite, English way. "Perhaps they don't like swimming."

"It's not normal. All kids like swimming."

"I never did." Nana Bea threw me into the deep end of the pool when I was really little and it scarred me for life.

Dawne smiled back. "But you're not American."

"What else?"

"They wouldn't play softball when we went to the park."

Personally, I'd never really been into contact sports since I got my ankle broken playing hockey. "Well, that doesn't seem like a big deal."

Dawne's smile became smug. "They totally refuse to take part in the camp play."

I began to say that a lot of children are shy, but Dawne cut me off.

"Because it's about Columbus discovering America, and Gallup says that Columbus wasn't a hero; he was a war criminal who slaughtered millions of people."

Gallup and Tampa materialized at my side.

"It's true," said Tampa.

**124**

Gallup, of course, provided the details. "Six years after Columbus landed, three million natives were dead."

Dawne gave me a look. "See what I mean?"

I reckoned Gallup was probably right – all the other explorers slaughtered millions of people, so why not Columbus?

I said, "But what if it is true?"

"I can't have it," said Dawne. "They're giving the other kids ideas. Half of them wouldn't eat their hot dogs the other day because Gallup told everyone they had pig ears in them."

"Gallup thinks everything has pig ears in it," said Tampa. "Unless it's a vegetable."

Gallup was a natural outsider – as I now was. It gave us a bond. I put a hand on his shoulder. "Gallup's a very committed vegetarian."

I might as well have said he was a very committed communist.

"That's what I mean," said Dawne. "I'm going to have a revolution on my hands if this keeps up."

I smiled sweetly. "And wouldn't that be typically American."

# Home Alone

Gallup and Tampa couldn't have been happier if they'd just been released from jail.

"I didn't like it there anyway," said Gallup. "They have a rabbit in a tiny little cage."

I said I was surprised he hadn't tried to rescue it.

"I was going to," he said. "But Dawne was always watching me because of last year."

I didn't ask. One had to admire his spirit.

"I didn't like it either," said Tampa. "It was like being in the army."

"Is that because of the uniforms?" I asked. "Or the long marches?"

"Because they want everybody to be just the same," she said.

They weren't the only ones who took this change of plan in their stride.

"There goes the free lunch," said Mrs Salamanca. "I should've known it wouldn't last." She sighed. "But it's not all bad news, is it, Soph?" I'd given up trying to get her to call me by my name. "Now you have someone to see all the sights with."

"I didn't think there'd be much left to see." I smiled politely. "I mean, we did do the tour."

"Oh, there's tons." Mrs Salamanca started ticking off the tons of things left to see on her fingers. "There's the museum, and the aquarium, and the zoo and the library, and the park, and the botanical gardens... And that's just around here. After that you've got Manhattan."

"Well," I said. "I'm still getting used to things."

"If you take much longer to get used to things you'll be back in London before you ever get over the bridge." She clamped a hand on my shoulder. "You know, I've been a little worried about you staying in all the time, Soph. I'd hoped you'd do some exploring. Sitting in the house isn't much of a vacation."

I hadn't told Mrs Salamanca about my doomed expedition to buy a fan before and I wasn't going to tell her now. "Oh, I'm fine in the house. It's too hot to go out anyway."

"It'll be a lot hotter inside with those two," she warned. "It's not a good idea to have them in a confined space. You have to keep them busy."

By the end of only one day on my own with Tampa and Gallup I knew that Mrs Salamanca was right. They wouldn't even watch telly for hours on end like normal children.

Gallup was obsessed with wildlife documentaries and bored by everything else, and if there
wasn't some programme about wombats or killer
sharks on he'd chase Bart and Bill around the
house to give them exercise.

"Bart's a pig," I said. "He's meant to be fat."

"Not if he isn't going to be chopped up for
bacon, he isn't," said Gallup.

"Well, Bill's an iguana. I don't believe they're
meant to be long-distance runners."

"He needs to keep in shape. In case he's ever
imprisoned again."

Tampa liked telly even less than her brother.
After half an hour she claimed her eyes hurt and
insisted I play cards with her. She cheated. Not
only that but her favourite game was War – which
was not my favourite. When I refused to play any
more she stood in the sitting room imitating a train
on her violin. It was enough to drive one mad.

That's why I decided to clean the house. I reckoned this would kill not one but five birds with a
single stone. It would keep Gallup busy; it would
keep Tampa busy; it would keep me busy; it would
help Mrs Salamanca sort out her life (and God
knows she needed help); and it didn't require
leaving the house.

It seemed to me that the problem with both Mrs
Salamanca's life and her children was that neither
seemed to be very organized. Nana Bea says anything can be organized so long as you have rules,
so I made rules for Gallup and Tampa.

They weren't to think I was a servant to wait on them and keep them entertained. They had to play in the back garden unless it was raining or there was a health warning out about the air.

"So let's go to the park," said Tampa. "You can use Cherokee's bike."

I was not going to a park where domestic fowl were sacrificed in dark rituals, not even in daylight.

"Barbee can come too," said Gallup.

And what good would that do? It was pretty obvious that Barbee couldn't protect herself – never mind anyone else.

"And Will," added Tampa.

"Will?"

Tampa could also sigh like Mrs Salamanca. "That's the baby."

"Oh," I said. "Of course. But in any event it's much too hot to go cycling. I'm sweating enough as it is. And the ba— Will shouldn't be out in all this heat. He's far too young."

Tampa gave me one of her looks. "Don't English people go outside?"

"Of course we go outside. We're fanatical walkers." I gave her a look back. "Unlike some people. If you ask me the Scutaris' sign should say JESUS WALKED, not ask what kind of car he'd own."

Tampa's expression didn't change. "But the English don't ride bikes?"

I informed her that the English invented the bicycle.

Gallup shook his head. "Actually, the first

treadle-propelled bike was made by a Scottish guy."

"There's plenty to do right here," I said. "I thought you wanted to make a run for Bart in the garden. You could do that."

They had to help keep the house tidy.

"What's that mean?" asked Tampa.

"Keep it neat."

"But we can't keep it neat," Gallup argued. "It's not neat now."

I patted his head. "Oh, but it will be."

This was the master stroke of my plan: I was going to put the Casa Salamanca in some sort of order. Nothing too drastic, of course. As much as I would have liked to get a skip and throw everything out, I knew I had to content myself with the basics. No more dishes in the sink. No more bendy carrots in the fridge. No more cartons of juice with foreign objects floating in them. No more cobwebs. No more dust bunnies. No more heaps of old plastic bags, jars, bottles, tins, boxes and labels. No more underwear or decaying food on the floor. No more avalanches when one opened a cupboard.

I worked like a woman possessed. I hoovered. I dusted. I cleaned the windows and polished the furniture. I stuck incense in the hall to discourage Pancho Villa from using it as a loo. I made sure that there was a drawer where anything that was used regularly would be safe from the Pig Who Would Eat Brooklyn.

Mrs Salamanca noticed the difference on night one.

"Good grief." She stood in the hallway, sniffing. "It doesn't smell like urine." Her eyes moved round the sitting room. "And I can see out the windows!"

She said I shouldn't have. She said it was enough that I was stuck with the kids.

I said it was my way of saying thank you for everything.

I reached the hall cupboard on Friday. I felt like Hercules mucking out the Augean stables. By the afternoon I had everything out – and I mean everything. There were all the usual things one expects to find in a hall cupboard – wellies, coats, scarves, jackets, hats, umbrellas, an unopened smoke alarm – but there were also all the things the Salamancas thought belonged there. I found blankets, three torches that didn't work, an axe, boxes of broken plates and cups, bags of old bottles and jars, a crate full of old toys, several metal signs, a rusted ice pick, bamboo ski poles, an old tricycle, a brand new fondue dish, three cat carriers, an ancient pair of ice skates, a bee-keeper's bonnet and a paddling pool. I was just about to take the paddling pool out into the garden when the doorbell rang.

It was Barbee and Will.

Barbee held up the neon-pink object she was holding in the hand that wasn't holding the baby. "We brought you a fan. It took me a while to find it because it was buried in the cellar."

Pink is a favourite colour of mine, but not in neon – and not on a fan.

"Oh," I said. "I mean, thank you. That's really kind, but Mrs Salamanca thinks there may be one in the loft." Though no one had yet been brave or desperate enough to look, because opening the hatch was like opening the door of a roaring furnace.

"The what?" Barbee smiled uncertainly. "Are you talking in English?"

It did seem to be a habit of mine. "You know…" Good Lord, what did they call it? "On top of the house but under the roof."

"Oh!" I hadn't realized Barbee wore braces before. "You mean the attic."

"Right," I said. "The attic."

"Well, use this till you find it." Barbee managed to wave the fan and stop the baby from gouging out her eye at the same time. "This one has five speeds."

Despite the fact that I had one of Cherokee's bandannas wrapped around my head, was dirty as a mechanic and was obviously busy, Barbee stood there waiting for me to invite her in.

I didn't want to. I was certain Barbee with her fan was like the Trojans and their wooden horse – once she got her foot in the door I'd never get rid of her. But what could I do? With her bunches of hair and her baby drooling on her shoulder she looked like a little kid who'd come over to play.

"Would you like to come in?"

Barbee's face lit up as if someone had just plugged her in. "Sure." She thrust the fan into my hands. "That'd be great."

"Go into the kitchen." I held open the door. "We've got lemonade."

"Jeepers." Barbee stepped over the piles of things in the hall. "What's goin' on? Don't tell me Jake's finally being evicted."

"Not yet. I'm just doing some cleaning."

We put the fan on the kitchen table and the baby on a blanket on the floor.

I asked Barbee if she wanted some biscuits.

"What? With lemonade?" She gave me another look at her braces. "I usually have them with gravy."

"Cookies," I corrected myself, and took the box out of the cupboard.

Barbee preferred toast.

I gave her the toaster and the bread. She didn't want butter; she wanted catsup. Welcome to Brooklyn – the Other World.

We talked about the weather while I got the lemonade and the catsup out of the fridge. We talked about Will's nappy rash – which apparently was really gruesome because of the heat – while I poured the lemonade into glasses.

"He's a very cute baby," I said.

"Yeah," said Barbee. "He's OK, ain't he? At least he's got all his toes and stuff."

"How—" I stopped short.

**133**

"How what?" asked Barbee.

"Nothing." I could feel myself blushing. "It's none of my business." Living with the Salamancas was obviously starting to fuddle my mind.

"How'd I end up with Will?" Barbee smiled. "It was easy. I got pregnant."

"Did—"

"Did I do it on purpose?" Barbee shifted Will back onto his blanket. "Not really. I was gonna finish school first. But Fidel's really happy."

I stopped in the act of taking a biscuit. "Pardon?" The only person I knew named Fidel was the leader of Cuba.

"That's Will's dad."

"Fidel Castro is Will's dad?"

"Of course not!" Barbee's bunches all bobbed. "He's not one of them. He's Colombian. Fidel Casamayor. He's in the army. He's training to be a mechanic. So if he doesn't want to stay in the army and maybe get shot he can always get a good job."

"Oh. In the army."

"That's why we decided to get married. So when he goes somewhere you can bring wives, he can send for me and Will."

I'd been so convinced that Barbee was a gymslip mum that it surprised me more to discover that she was married than it had to find out she had a child. "You're married?"

"Sure." Barbee giggled. "What'd you think?"

"Well, it's just that … in England…"

"People don't get married? I never knew that."

**134**

"No, of course they get married. It's just – oh, never mind."

Barbee knew a bit about Britain – she'd heard of the royal family, Tony Blair, the Beatles and the Spice Girls, and she knew we drank tea – but her knowledge of Europe was more vague.

Barbee laughed. "Of course I know where Europe is." She waved towards the east. "It's over there. That's where they had the Second World War."

I didn't want her to think that was the only thing we should be remembered for.

"It's where a lot of people in this country came from," I reminded her.

"Not me," said Barbee. "I was born here."

She knew that Rome is in Italy because "that's where the Pope lives" and she knew that Paris is in France because "everybody knows that" – but she wasn't sure about Madrid or Berlin and she had never heard of Prague.

"But some day you might be living in Europe," I reminded her. "You know, if Fidel gets posted to Germany or something. Aren't you curious about what it's like?"

"We'll live on the base," said Barbee. "And anyway I know they've got McDonald's."

I didn't know what to talk about next. Not school, obviously. I gazed at the drool and milk stains on Barbee's T-shirt. Not clothes.

"Mrs Salamanca isn't really going to get evicted, is she?" I asked as I put the glasses on the table and sat down across from her.

"Who knows?" Barbee picked up her drink with a shrug. "Jake's always behind with the rent – plus her lease is coming up for renewal. Mom says the Big El's asking for more money. He'd love to get her out of here and the store. Then he could really jack up the prices."

"I don't see how he could do that." I passed her the plate of biscuits. "This place is practically falling down. I must trip on the pavement at least twice a day. And it's a wonder I haven't broken my neck on that railing."

Barbee shrugged again. "It's the law. Once Jake's out he can charge whatever he wants."

The sound of children's voices shrieking like sirens drifted towards us from the garden.

"So how come the kids are home?" asked Barbee. "I thought they were going to camp."

I told her what had happened.

"Heck, they lasted a week longer than—" Barbee broke off, nose twitching. "Is something burning?"

I raised my head and sniffed. Mingling with the lemon-fresh scent of the liquid cleaner I'd used on the kitchen and baby poo was the smell of burning wood. I got up and went to the window.

*"Oh my God!"*

There was a small bonfire roaring away in the middle of the garden – and it was starting to spread. Tampa and Gallup were running around, but I couldn't tell if they were trying to put it out or if they were just panicking. Once when Jocelyn and I were making fudge the oven glove caught fire and the two of us had run around so much we bumped into each other and fell over.

Barbee and the baby came up behind me. "Jeepers," said Barbee. "We better put that out."

I grabbed the phone and promptly dropped it. I retrieved it and punched in 999. Even though my heart was thudding so hard I could barely hear anything else, I could tell that that wasn't the number.

"Barbee! What do I dial for Emergency?"

But Barbee was already opening the back door – calmly.

"You don't need the fire department. Jake's got a hose." She shoved the baby at me. "Here. Take Will. I know where it is."

I watched her walk round the side of the house as though she was going to collect something she'd left there earlier, while the baby tried to rip the gold hoop out of my ear.

"Hey, you guys!" Barbee shouted. "Help me with this hose!"

Gallup had wanted to see if he could start a fire by rubbing two sticks together as he'd seen it done in one of his documentaries. Obviously he could. What he couldn't do was control it.

Barbee, however, could. She might be a failure at practising birth control but she was definitely a dab hand at dealing with a crisis. By the time she was done all of us including the livestock were wet and sooty, but there wasn't so much as an ember still glowing on the lawn.

"I better get Will home." Barbee reached out her arms and he flung himself towards her. "He looks like I made him sleep in the fireplace."

"I can't thank you enough," I said. "You were absolutely brilliant."

Barbee was philosophical. "I have brothers. This stuff happens all the time."

I was still thanking her as I followed her into the hall.

She stepped over a bag of empty jars. "You know, my dad's taking stuff to the recycling place tomorrow if you want to get rid of some of this."

"I do. That's a good idea."

"So," said Barbee when we reached the door. "You wanna do something together on Monday? Since we both have kids?"

I didn't hesitate. How could I say no? If it hadn't been for her the highlight of my summer would have been burning down the house.

"Sure. That would be brilliant."

"Great." Barbee started down the steps.

That's what happens when you can't thank someone enough.

# Destructo Pig Strikes Again

Aside from some superficial similarities common to the human species – hands with thumbs, two legs, upright posture, the ability to cry, et cetera – Barbee was *nothing* like my friends back in London. She had no hobbies, no interests, no fashion skills, no ambition, and she couldn't find Portugal on a map of Europe. On the other hand, she was better in an emergency (when the oven glove caught on fire that time, Jocelyn finally ran into the garden) and there was no danger that (had I had either) Barbee would lose my mobile or steal my boyfriend. With Barbee Casamayor, what you saw was what you got. My friends back home might have been a lot smarter than Barbee, but they were also more complicated – one day they'd say you were like a sister to them and the next they'd be looking for some sharp implement to stick in your back.

Barbee and I got into the habit of taking Gallup,

Tampa and Will to the park in the afternoons. Tampa would ride her bike; Gallup would look for animals, birds and insects to rescue; Will would do what babies do, which isn't that much and usually involved having to be cleaned up afterwards; and Barbee and I would get ices from the ice cream van and talk.

I found out that the Scutari men were all in construction, Mrs Scutari worked part-time as a doctor's receptionist, Mr Scutari once came home so drunk that Mrs Scutari found his boots in the loo in the morning, George's scar was not from a knife fight but from falling on a nail, and Barbee sometimes made extra money waiting tables. I also found out that you should always be nice to your waiter because he or she really might spit in your dinner, Julia Roberts was Barbee's favourite actress even though she didn't shave under her arms, the United States was the alien abductions capital of the world, the United States won the Second World War (for us), there were at least twenty-seven certified manias and Barbee reckoned she knew someone with each of them, and Jesus will probably be born in Wyoming next time.

And then Bart ate the plug off the pink fan.

"I'll buy you a new one," I promised. It was the least I could do.

"No sweat," said Barbee. "We can take it up to the hardware store and they'll fix it. Mr Bachman knows all about Bart."

The five of us walked up the avenue to the

hardware store I'd never noticed before because I was always so busy trying to get off the road.

Gallup opened the door and he and Tampa charged through. Barbee was next – pushing Will – and I brought up the rear, carrying the fan. Because I was behind the others I was already at the counter before I saw him.

"Barbee!" I grabbed her arm. "Barbee – it's *him*!"

She looked round. "Him who?"

"That bloke I told you about. The one who followed me home that time." And I couldn't even hide behind Cherokee's sunglasses because Bart had eaten them. It was no wonder Mrs Salamanca never bought anything new.

Barbee's bunches bobbed as her head swung back and forth. "Where?"

"There! Behind the counter."

"That's not a bloke." Barbee laughed. "That's Bachman."

"That's Mr Bachman? He told me his name was Bobby."

"Not Mr Bachman. That's his son." Barbee bobbed some more. "Bobby Bachman."

"Oh," I said. "I thought he was a psycho."

"Nah. He's a friend of Cherokee's."

"Friend? As in boyfriend?" Judging by her wardrobe it was more than possible. I wondered how she kissed him without getting caught in his nose-ring.

She shrugged. "I don't think so." She shrugged

again. "Maybe." Another shrug. "I don't know."

"Let's forget about this." I tugged on her arm. "I'll come back some other time."

"But we're here now." Barbee might not be the brightest ornament on the tree, but she was logical. "It'll only take a minute."

I can't say that Bobby Bachman looked any better to me now that I knew he didn't live in a squat. If anything, he looked worse. He was wearing a vest T-shirt so the tattoos on his arms were visible. A lot of the boys I knew back in London were into grunge – and they might even wear an earring or have a small tattoo somewhere discreet – but they were deeply normal and destined to be upstanding members of society (or at least corporate solicitors). Bobby Bachman was more likely to be a member of a rebel army. He was still to be avoided the way my ancestors avoided the plague. I crossed my fingers and prayed he wouldn't recognize me.

Which was ridiculous, of course. I might as well have had a neon sign flashing on and off over my head. Gallup and Tampa were already screaming hello.

He came over to us straight away. "Well, if it isn't the English girl." He gave me a big grin. "I figured you fled the country."

"She thought you were going to kill her," Barbee explained. "She's real nervous. I practically had to drag her to the park the first time."

Bachman said he'd been meaning to drop by and

142

see how I was doing, but he'd been pretty busy. Apparently his old man worked him like a slave.

"Thanks," I said. "That's very kind of you." I gestured to Gallup and Tampa, who were both behind the counter by now, annoying the dog, whose name seemed to be Bruce Lee. "But I'm pretty busy myself."

"Maybe we could go for a bike ride one evening," he said as he fitted the new plug onto the fan. "Show you the sights."

"I've seen them," I said. Barbee stepped on my foot. I laughed. "Both of them."

"Is that a no?"

"Of course not. I mean, I…" I was about to say that I couldn't ride a bicycle, but then I realized that even Will was watching me. Will was the only one who hadn't seen me ride Gallup's bike the day before, because he'd been asleep. "I don't want to be any trouble."

"No trouble." He shoved the fan across the counter. "I'll give you a call."

As far as I was concerned he could call all he wanted – that didn't mean I had to answer.

# Twenty Minutes from Brooklyn

Mrs Salamanca finally sorted out the problem of my missing luggage. She heard me on the phone one morning trying to discover where my case was now.

"I'm sorry to be such a nuisance," I was saying. "But this has been going on for quite a while."

Mrs Salamanca appeared beside me wiping toast crumbs from her mouth with the sleeve of the bowling shirt she was wearing. There were motorcycles swinging from her ears. "Give me."

"It's all right," I whispered. "I—"

She whipped the receiver out of my hand.

"Hello? My name's Jacqueline Salamanca. I want to speak to your supervisor."

I gently tapped her on the shoulder. "Mrs Sala—"

She gave me a shove and turned her back on me.

Mrs Salamanca told the supervisor that unless they'd sent my luggage to Mars she couldn't see any reason why the only place it hadn't been in the last few weeks was Brooklyn. She said she thought the newspapers would be interested in the story, and that she not only expected the bag to be delivered within the next twenty-four hours but she expected me to be compensated for my time, expense and inconvenience as well.

My bag still didn't rematerialize – but I had a cheque for five hundred dollars in my hand the following day.

"The squeaky wheel gets the grease," said Mrs Salamanca.

Barbee said she'd go shopping with me to get some new gear. "I've got money saved from my birthday, but I have nobody to go with. It's no fun shopping just with Will."

Mrs Scutari was volunteered to look after everybody's children on one of her days off.

"That's brilliant." I didn't bother to try to hide my excitement. I was feeling pretty confident about swanning around now – especially since I had a mate to swan around with. At last I was going to see Manhattan. Look out, Fifth Avenue, here I come! "We can go into the city as soon as the rush hour's over."

Barbee frowned. "The city? You mean Manhattan?"

You'd think she'd just arrived from Tibet.

"Of course I mean Manhattan. People come from Japan to shop in Manhattan. Julia Roberts shops in Manhattan."

"I don't go into the city," said Barbee.

I thought she was joking. "Of course you don't."

Barbee's bunches bobbed. "No, really. We went to see the tree at the Rockefeller Center when I was little, and once I went with my mom and her bridge club to see *Cats*, but otherwise I never go."

I couldn't decide what surprised me more – that Barbee lived twenty minutes by tube from New York and never went there or that Mrs Scutari belonged to a bridge club.

"But why not?"

Barbee shrugged. "What for?"

"What for? You mean aside from the fact that it's the cultural capital of the world?"

"It's full of weirdos and thieves. You don't want to know the stories I've heard."

I pretended to yawn. "They can't be any worse than the ones I've heard."

"But we've got everything anybody needs right here in Brooklyn."

"But what about the museums, the galleries, the theatres, the shops…"

Barbee pointed out that Brooklyn had shops. "And a museum, and galleries, and there's a truck they have plays in, and a zoo."

"But, Barbee," I pleaded, "I really want to see the city. I can't come three thousand miles and never even see the Empire State Building."

"You can see it from Brooklyn Heights," said Barbee.

"But not Broadway. I can't see Broadway from Brooklyn Heights."

"There's nothing to see unless you want to get mugged," she assured me. "We saw someone get her purse snatched on Broadway when we went to see the tree."

"Barbee, please… I'm begging you. I don't want to go on my own."

She crossed her arms and scowled – which made her look about eight. Her bunches were practically dancing by now. "It's too dangerous."

"It can't be. People live there. People with babies."

"I don't think my folks would let me."

"But you're a married woman."

"But I still live with my folks, don't I?"

I gave reason the boot and opted for bribery. "Tell you what," I said. "I'll treat you to lunch – and pay your fare."

She stopped bobbing. "Really? We'll have lunch out?" She frowned. "But not at McDonald's, right? My mom takes me there all the time."

I immediately agreed. "Not McDonald's – some trendy New York café like you see in films. Somewhere Julia Roberts would have lunch."

But she was still frowning. "What if we get lost?"

"We won't get lost," I promised. "I'll get a map."

Mrs Salamanca not only gave me a map, she made a list of places to visit and things to see and

**147**

marked them all in purple highlighter.

"You don't want to go above Fourteenth Street unless you're going to the museum or Central Park."

"I don't?" I wasn't certain if Fifth Avenue was above Fourteenth Street or not.

She reacted as if I'd said I wanted to go to Antarctica. "Fifth Avenue? Why would you want to go there?"

"To shop?"

"Oh, Soph… You don't want to go to Fifth Avenue."

I didn't?

"Fifth Avenue's a major drag. People only shop there if they have more money than brains and need someone else to tell them how to dress. Downtown has much more character and history – and the best stores. You can get some really cool things – and they're not ten times the price they should be."

Mrs Salamanca said to take the F train. Barbee was armed with her mobile phone and a personal alarm, and I was armed with Mrs Salamanca's map and personal itinerary.

"Are you sure you know where to get off?" Barbee whispered as the train doors closed behind us.

I'd committed it to memory. "Broadway-Lafayette," I whispered back. "South-west exit, turn left."

I started to sit down. "Not there!" hissed Barbee.

"You want to sit in the middle so they can't grab your bag as they're getting off the train."

The other passengers were several women with children, a couple of girls our age, and two middle-aged men reading newspapers. I wasn't sure who "they" were meant to be.

"I don't have a bag," I reminded her. I had my money in my purse belt.

"OK, so they can't stab you as they leave the train," amended Barbee.

We sat in the middle of the carriage. I glanced around.

"Don't make eye contact with anyone," she whispered. "We should've brought books."

I'd never seen Barbee read anything except the TV guide.

"Stop winding me up," I ordered. "We're meant to be having fun, remember?"

"Um." Barbee stared at the ground.

The train left the tunnel and clattered over Brooklyn, past factories and shops; past advertisements for insurance, cars and Jesus; past traffic jams and houses with decks and pools and barbecues in the backyards.

And then I saw something I wasn't expecting at all. It was a bit like riding down the Westway and seeing a pyramid nestled in among the tower blocks.

"Good Lord." I poked Barbee. "Look at that!"

Barbee tore her eyes from the toes of her trainers to see the enormous figure of a woman rising

149

above the patio umbrellas and the lorries, her torch held high as if to say, "*Come shop!* You're safe with me."

Barbee craned her neck. "Is that the Statue of Liberty?"

"That or a very good copy."

"Gee," she said. "I didn't know you could see her from the F train."

Live and learn, as Daddy would say.

No one else paid any more attention to that symbol of hope and freedom than they were paying to the possibility of being mugged – they were all either reading or half asleep – but Barbee started to relax.

"Did you know you used to be able to climb up to her crown?" she asked. "I always wanted to do that, but I don't like heights. One time I got stuck up a jungle gym and my brother had to carry me down. I was *so* embarrassed I thought I'd die."

I laughed. "Embarrassed? That's nothing." I told her about going up to the top of the Tower of London and how I threw up on Mummy. "But it wasn't the height or anything. I just didn't feel well."

We started chatting as if we were back in Prospect Park. In fact we got so involved in swapping stories of embarrassing moments of the past that we nearly missed our stop.

"Good Lord!" I grabbed Barbee's hand and yanked her out of her seat. "Broadway-Lafayette."

After a few minutes of confusion (and the help

of a bloke who was blessing everybody and begging for change) we located the south-west exit.

In anticipation of my first glimpse of New York that wasn't from a distance, I held my breath as we reached the top of the stairs leading to the street. Which was just as well. It was so hot you could see the pollution in the gaps between the rushing crowd.

"Gee ... there's sure a lot of people, isn't there?" Barbee slipped her arm through mine. "I don't want to lose you."

I already had Mrs Salamanca's directions in my hand. "We go left," I said. I didn't particularly want to lose her either.

The first shop on Mrs Salamanca's list was exactly where she said it would be.

We stepped inside.

Barbee looked round as though it were her first trip off the farm. "Do you have stores like this in London?"

"I don't think so. Not in Putney." It was the size of an aeroplane hangar and spread over three sprawling levels. From what I could see it sold everything from vintage clothes to designer labels and shoes to hats. "Not under one roof."

"We always go to the mall," said Barbee. "But this is nothing like Macy's."

It was nothing like Top Shop, or Hennes, or Miss Selfridge, either. Maybe this wasn't such a good idea after all.

I turned to Barbee. "I'm not sure I'm going to

find anything that suits me here."

"Huh?" Barbee smiled the way she did when I talked in English. "What do you mean?"

"You know." Beside us was a display of dungarees dyed in outrageous colours. "I don't think they have anything that's really me."

Barbee glanced from me to the dungarees and back again. "It looks like you to me."

"Really?" I stared beyond the rails of clothes to the mirrored wall behind them. Since I usually had about three minutes in the bathroom – where the largest mirror in the house lived – and since I was usually concentrating on not stepping into the cat litter tray, I hadn't really seen myself for a while. I wore my hair clipped up all the time now because of the heat and so that Will didn't wrench it out by the roots. In Cherokee's black combat trousers and her purple T-shirt with the black stars and my hair sticking up all over my head, I didn't look like me any more. I looked like a funky New Yorker.

"Come on," I said. "Shoes first. I'm tired of looking at my big toe."

Our confidence grew as we shopped. We bought tops and skirts, jeans, shoes, socks, underwear and fake CK sunglasses from a street vendor, an iguana T-shirt for Gallup, violin socks for Tampa and even a miniature motorcycle jacket for Will. By the time we were ready for lunch we were so confident that we decided to venture over to the East Side to the restaurant recommended by Mrs Salamanca. Heads up and strides wide, we crossed several major thoroughfares till we came to an intersection where roads went off in every direction. It was almost like a roundabout.

"Straight ahead," I decided.

Barbee peered over the top of her new sunglasses. "But which way is that?"

I pointed to the road slightly to the right. "That way."

It was Barbee who noticed our mistake first.

"This is wrong," she said. She pushed her glasses up on her head. "It can't be down here."

"Why not?"

"Why not?" She glanced around us. Warily. Unhappily. Without focusing on anything. "You're kidding me, right? In these buildings?"

She did have a point. The buildings in question were tall, brick, covered with graffiti and rundown in a threatening sort of way.

"It looks like an estate."

Barbee snorted. "Yeah, right. Like rich people would live somewhere like this."

"Not that sort of estate. A housing estate." The sort where the residents were terrorized by drug dealers and gangs.

"Oh, you mean a project." Barbee lowered her voice. "Yeah, this is a project. You know – for really poor people."

"We must have come down the wrong street." I started to take out the map Mrs Salamanca had drawn for me.

"Don't do that," she hissed. "Everyone'll know that we're lost."

"But we *are* lost."

"Yeah, but we don't want them to know it."

This time I knew who "them" were. "Them" were the men slouching about who could be either drug dealers or gang members.

Her voice wobbled. "That's how tourists become crime victims."

We'd definitely come to the end of a perfect day.

The old me, raised by Caroline Pitt-Turnbull, would have panicked. But the old me hadn't travelled Flatbush Avenue on her own or liberated a tree iguana. The new me had.

"Right," I said. "Well, what about your phone? We could ring Jake and—"

"Take out my phone? Here? Are you nuts?"

Several of the men who were slouching about were watching us now with unconcealed interest.

"Why did you bring it if you won't use it?"

"For an emergency."

"And this isn't an emergency?"

"It'll be a tragedy if I let them see my phone, that's what it'll be." I'd never noticed before how much like Will she looked when she was upset. "I knew I shouldn't have let you talk me into coming with you. Now we're going to be murdered or something and Will'll grow up without a mother and become a heroin addict and ruin his life and Fidel will get himself shot in some foreign country because he has nothing to live for and—"

"Oh, for heaven's sake." She was reminding me of Mummy. I'd always thought Mummy's ability to think of all the things that might go wrong in any situation was a display of her thoughtfulness and concern, but that wasn't how it was striking me now. Now it seemed more like being paralysed by fear. Sometimes you just had to get on with things. "Stop panicking, will you? All we have to do is go back the way we came."

"And how do we know what that is?"

This was another good point. We'd been forced to do a bit of meandering after that fateful intersection.

"We'll ask someone."

Don't panic... All we have to do... Ask someone... I almost couldn't believe this was *me* speaking.

Barbee couldn't believe it either.

"*Ask* someone?"

"Sure." There was a small grocery shop across the road. "We'll ask in there."

Barbee took hold of my arm. "I'll follow you."

We weren't that far off – just one block too far south and two blocks too far east.

"You see?" I said as we headed for the restaurant a second time. "Easy-peasy."

We sat in the garden at a table with an umbrella. There was a parrot chained to a perch in one corner, a woman playing the saxophone in another, a fountain in the middle of the courtyard, and a table of transvestites.

155

"This is really cool," said Barbee. "I've never been anywhere like this before."

Neither had I. Oh, if only my friends could see me now.

We were in high spirits as we headed back to the F train. We laughed and swung our carrier bags as we strolled through Washington Square Park. We sailed into the station and through the turnstile. We clattered down the steps to the platform as though we'd been riding the F train to Brooklyn all our lives.

Someone who probably had been riding the F train to Brooklyn all his life was leaning against a metal pillar watching the mice running in the tracks. He must have heard my accent, because he looked up even before we reached the platform.

"I don't believe it." He made the face of a boy who suddenly sees a camel coming down the subway steps. "Barbee Casamayor left Brooklyn? Did I miss a blue moon or something?"

Barbee laughed. "Get outta here."

He grinned at me. "I was gonna call you later. See if you want to do something Sunday."

The moment I'd been dreading since he fixed the fan. I'd even made Gallup and Tampa swear that if he called and they answered, they would tell him I was out. And here I was, caught like a rabbit in the headlamps of a car. Not a nanosecond of hesitation slowed my response.

"Sure," I said. "That'd be brilliant."

My spirits were well out of control.

# My Night on the Town

Bachman took Gallup, Tampa, Barbee, Will and me to Central Park to see the horse-drawn cabs and the place where John Lennon was shot (Gallup got into a rather heated discussion about horse rights with a cabby and Barbee was sure she could still see a bloodstain, but Bachman said that didn't mean it was Lennon's blood; it could have been anybody's). He took us to the Museum of Modern Art (Will threw up and Tampa asked everyone in a uniform why her mother's work wasn't exhibited there). He took us to Grand Central Station to see the constellations on the ceiling (Barbee said she'd never seen so many stars and Tampa decided Jake should do the same thing in their sitting room). He took us to the Statue of Liberty (where Barbee looked up at the crown). He took us to the Museum of Natural History (we were thrown out in the end because Gallup couldn't be dragged away). He took Tampa, Gallup and me to the Museum

157

of the American Indian. He took us to Times Square, Chinatown and a shop on the Lower East Side that specialized in merchandise featuring either Elvis Presley or Jesus Christ (Bachman said it was the best Jesus and Elvis store on the planet).

Then one day Bachman invited me to the city again. But this was different. This was special. This wasn't in daylight. And this was just the two of us.

"Manhattan by moonlight," he said. "You can't leave till you've seen it. Not that you really will see the moon. But you'll know it's there."

I was overjoyed. As good as our expeditions had been, they hadn't exactly been glamorous. They went under the heading of Family Outings more than Exciting New York. Janice Freestone's aunt had gone sailing on the Long Island sound with FBI agents and business tycoons, not picnicking in Prospect Park. Milla Hewitt had eaten dinner in trendy restaurants where the person at the next table might be Brad Pitt or Milla Jovovich, not Chinese takeaway from round the corner. Polly Matthewman hadn't examined the horses' feet, instead she'd taken a cab round Central Park. Amy Lawson had had her photograph taken at a SoHo gallery, not with her head poking through a cardboard cut-out of the Statue of Liberty. Gemma Bloom had gone to so many celebrity fund-raisers she said she thought she should register as a charity. I wanted something to match all that.

"That'll be brilliant. Where will we go?"

158

And Bachman said (and I quote), "I thought we'd go bowling."

I was *taken aback*. *Taken aback* as in bowling is what you do in Jersey City, not New York. "Bowling? You want to go bowling?"

"You must've heard of bowling," said Bachman. "It comes from Europe."

"And that would be unlike what, precisely?"

"Unlike corn, tobacco, potatoes and the nuclear bomb."

I said that of course I'd heard of bowling; I just hadn't realized they had bowling alleys in New York. It wasn't really what one associated with the most cultural capital of the New World. Where would they put it?

"On Broadway. And it's right next door to one of the best Mexican restaurants north of *la línea*."

And who said Americans don't speak more than one language?

"*La* what?"

"The border."

I could hear my friends asking me what the most thrilling thing I had done in New York was, and I could hear myself saying that I went bowling and ate a burrito. I said, "Oh."

"Is this reluctance I sense because you don't know how to bowl?"

"No, it is not because I don't know how to bowl." I didn't want to hurt his feelings by telling him the truth. "It's just that Mummy said New York is dangerous at night—"

"Who cares what your mother said? She isn't here."

But Jake was. She was on the other side of the kitchen, looking for luminous paint in the broom cupboard. "Good Lord, Soph," she bellowed across the room, "you can't go home without having a night out in Manhattan. It'd be like going to Egypt and not seeing the pyramids."

"You see?" said Bachman.

"Besides," Jake continued, "you have nothing to worry about. You'll be with Bachman. He's a student of kung fu. Nothing'll happen to you with him."

The train broke down between stations before we were even out of Brooklyn.

I was fairly certain that nothing like this had ever happened to Polly, Amy, Gemma, Milla or Janice Freestone's aunt.

"Don't panic," said Bachman. "This happens all the time."

I smiled in an English sort of way. "That's so good to know." The truth was, considering the state of rail travel in Britain, where trains were always getting derailed or crashing into something, this didn't even register on my Richter scale of reasons to panic.

The tannoy crackled and someone with a heavy West Indian accent spoke.

"What's he saying?"

Bachman shrugged. "Your guess is as good as

mine. I don't think you're supposed to understand him; I think you're just supposed to be reassured that he's still there."

It was obvious from the way everyone was looking around that no one understood what was being said – and that they weren't all that reassured.

And then the power went out.

Bachman took his key chain from his pocket. Unlike Mummy, who simply worried and flapped, Bachman liked to be prepared for possible emergencies. Besides keys it held a Swiss army knife and a tiny torch. He turned on the torch.

"Oh goody," I said, "we can see the floor."

Someone – someone in the carriage, not someone at the controls – shouted, "Don't worry, folks. It'll be back on in a minute."

By the time the minute was up the carriage had turned into a sauna and a child had started to cry.

By the time ten minutes had passed people were starting to panic. It was hard to see exactly who was doing what, but more than one person was standing up and someone was banging on the doors.

"It's like honking your horn in a traffic jam," said Bachman. "What do they think's going to happen?"

It was beginning to smell as if we were in a cattle lorry.

A woman started shouting in Spanish.

"What is she saying?" I whispered to Bachman.

"She's from Colombia. She thinks we've been held up by guerrillas."

Once in primary school my teacher Miss Sawyer tried to show us what a chain reaction was by knocking over the first in a winding line of dominoes. It didn't work. One of the boys had let the class rabbit out of its cage, and before she could tap the first domino the rabbit landed in the middle of the line. On either side of the rabbit the dominoes stood as though they were cemented to the floor.

In contrast, the cries of *"Dios mío!"* set off a chain reaction that Miss Sawyer would have died for.

Everybody started yelling. I'm no linguist, but I was certain I could make out Russian and possibly Czech as well as Spanish.

I grabbed hold of Bachman. "Doesn't anybody speak English?"

"We're a melting pot, remember? You saw the Statue of Liberty: Give me your tired ... your hungry ... your poor... It doesn't say anything about what language they work in."

"Well, that's not like Britain. Our home secretary thinks immigrants should speak English even in their own homes."

Fortunately the power came back on before anyone fainted or broke a window. The train started to move.

*"Gracias a Dios!"* cried the woman from Colombia.

162

I seconded that.

"Bowling first," said Bachman. "You can't bowl on a full stomach."

The moment we stepped through the door I knew that since Nana Bea had never been to Paradise Lanes, she had no real idea what a right ballyhoo was. There was the usual racket made by the balls and the pins, but besides that everyone seemed to be shouting and screaming.

Our lane was sandwiched between two of the noisiest groups in the alley. If they weren't shrieking because someone had hit something, they were arguing about the scoring. Despite this ceaseless din, they seemed to be serious bowlers. The ones on the left were all in red shirts with their names in yellow stitching, and the ones on the right were in yellow with blue stitching.

Bachman made a spare first go.

"Gosh," I said. "Have you done this before?"

It was true that I could bowl, but only in the sense that Jocelyn's uncle took us all bowling for her twelfth birthday. I hadn't lost my touch, though. I threw into the gutter then, and I threw into the gutter now.

"Don't just plonk it down," coached Bachman. "Swing it."

What did he think I was trying to do?

"It's been a while," I said. "I'll do better next time."

Bachman did better. He got a strike.

I got another gutter ball.

163

On my next go Bachman came with me so he could show me what to do.

"This ball's all wrong," he decided. "It's way too heavy. No wonder you just drop it."

Then he made me practise before I actually let go. Back … step … step … dip … swing… All around us pins were dropping like autumn leaves. I felt as though everyone was watching me – and laughing. Watching and laughing. They could probably tell right off that I was English.

"All right," I said when I could take no more. "I think I've got it now."

Bachman went back to mission control. I took a deep breath. Back … step … step … dip … swing…

This time my ball didn't just roll over and die in the gutter. It flew through the air, bounced off the alley, leapt over the gutter and hit the two remaining pins in the lane on the left. I stifled a moan. Yet another thing that had never happened to Gemma, Polly, Amy, Milla or Janice Freestone's aunt.

Behind me, Bachman groaned out loud.

The man whose pins I'd knocked over moved faster than my ball had. According to his shirt his name was Jesus.

"Whaddayathinkyerdoin'?" he screamed.

"I'm sorry," I apologized. "I am so, so sorry. It was a total accident."

This did nothing to calm him down. He was practically puce with rage.

"I'd like to accident you. There oughta be a law.

**164**

You shouldn't be let in here!" And then he called me something Nana Bea calls her spaniel, Margaret, but never with the word "stupid" in front of it.

I started to stammer more apologies, when Bachman launched himself from his seat.

"Don't you talk to her like that!" he roared. "Apologize to her. She's a guest in this country."

This had the effect of turning Jesus's anger on him. "She ain't *my* guest! *My* guests know how to bowl."

I repeated how sorry I was. "I'm so, so, so sorry. If there's some way I can make it up to you…"

But Jesus wasn't listening to me. He and Bachman were too busy making threatening gestures and shouting at each other. Now everyone really was watching us.

I was *totally humiliated. Totally humiliated* as in someone was going to call the police and we were going to be arrested, which was another thing that had never happened to Gemma, Polly, Amy, Milla or Janice Freestone's aunt.

In films when blokes get into a fight like that, one of them will ask the other if he wants to step outside. But I suspected from the way Jesus seemed to be growing in size and the way Bachman was poking him in the chest that that moment had passed.

I had to do something. What I wanted to do was leave, but I didn't think much of my chances of getting back to Brooklyn on my own. I took a very deep breath and pushed myself between them.

"You can stop this nonsense right now!" I informed them in my best impersonation of Nana Bea telling off a salesperson or traffic warden. "Stop acting like two-year-olds. For heaven's sake, it's only a bleeding game."

Jesus stopped yelling and looked at me as though I'd just clobbered him with a wet fish.

"Oi," he said. "Where are you from?"

Although we all parted friends amid laughter and questions about the Queen, Bachman and I decided not to play a second game. I was too shattered and Bachman was too hungry.

"There's nothing like a little naked aggression to give you an appetite," he said.

The restaurant was small and decorated with tin birds and paper flowers. There was a large photograph surrounded by fairy lights of an unsmiling, moustachioed man in a glittering black sombrero on the far wall. I thought he must be a bullfighter.

"Emiliano Zapata," explained Bachman. "You could say he fought bulls, but they were the human kind."

"The food must be good," I said as we squeezed ourselves into a corner. "The waiters all look like they come from Mexico."

Bachman laughed. "Nah. They all come from Queens."

I stared at my menu. "Bachman, it's in Spanish." "Flip it over."

Our waiter may have come from Queens but

his grasp of English didn't include my accent.

"*Qué?*" he kept saying. "*Qué? Qué?*"

Even pointing didn't help.

"*Qué? Qué? Qué?*"

I felt as if I were in an episode of *Fawlty Towers*. I could only hope it wasn't the one where the rat popped up from the biscuit tin.

In the end, Bachman ordered for me. He chose the vegetarian combination plates: two cheese enchiladas, rice and refried beans.

"*Y lo mismo para mí,*" said Bachman. "*Sí, fuerte.*"

I assumed that meant fast – as in before he started on the tablecloth.

We ate tortilla chips and salsa and got hysterical recounting our adventures on the train and in the bowling alley.

"You're gonna like this," Bachman assured me as the waiter set our meals in front of us.

He was almost right. The first bite was heaven. The second was *hell*. *Hell* as in it set my mouth on fire. What were the chances that this had ever happened to Gemma, Polly, Amy, Milla or Janice Freestone's aunt?

"Oh my God! Oh my God!" Even to my ears I sounded like someone in a disaster film when things start to go horribly wrong. Everyone was looking at us again. I made a grab for my glass of water and knocked it off the table.

"Just as well," commented Bachman. "Dry food works better."

As if he'd heard him, a waiter came rushing over with a plate with a piece of bread on it.

Our waiter was right behind him. "Too hot? Too hot?" he asked. "Too hot? Too hot?"

"It's my fault," said Bachman. "I told him to make it hot."

I was choking and nodding, but speech was beyond me.

"I bring other," said the waiter, and he whisked my plate away.

The manager came over. I reckoned he was worried I was going to sue them like that woman who sued McDonald's because her coffee was hot.

He wanted to know if I was all right.

"I'm fine," I managed to gasp. "It was just a wee bit spicy for me."

"Hey," said the manager. "Where're you from?"

I told him where I was from.

Understanding lit up his face. "Oh, English!" He said our meals were on the house.

"Thank you," I said as we stepped out into the rain that had started falling while we were inside. "I thought one of us might die a couple of times, but on the whole I have had a really brilliant time."

"It's not over yet," said Bachman. "I've saved the best for last."

"Really?" Perhaps I was going to have something they'd recognize to tell my friends after all. "Where are we going?"

Bachman said (and I quote), "The Staten Island Ferry."

"We're going to Staten Island?" I wasn't even certain where it was.

He shook his head. "Nah, we're just going on the ferry."

Bachman insisted that we stay inside by the snack bar, facing Staten Island, on the way out. He didn't want to ruin the surprise.

I rather felt I'd had enough surprises for one night. "What surprise?"

"You'll see."

Everyone else got off when we docked, which made me a little nervous. "Are you sure it's going back?" I didn't want the surprise to be a night on an empty boat.

"Pretty sure."

Eventually a few people trickled on board. The ferry groaned into action.

"Come on," he said. "You don't want to miss any of this.

"But I haven't finished my drink."

"Bring it with you."

Bachman and I stood on the deck, clutching our paper cups, while the ferry chugged through the downpour.

"It's raining in my Coke," I grumbled.

"Don't look in your Coke," ordered Bachman. "Look out there."

Out there was the city of Manhattan, lit up like a million Christmas trees. I was *stunned*. *Stunned* as in none of my friends had seen anything like this.

"My God! I feel like we're going to Oz."

"Didn't I tell you you'd like it?" Bachman put an arm round my shoulder. "Cheapest thrill in New York."

# Just When You Think It's Safe to Go into the Water...

So all's well that ends well, right? Happy endings all round.

Not in Brooklyn. Brooklyn's got its own plot.

I came back one Saturday night from a meal in Chinatown with Bachman to find that Jake had taken everything out of the cupboard in the hallway. She was sitting on the floor, surrounded by bags and boxes. She looked the way people always look on the news after they've been bombed out of their homes.

"Jake!" I dropped my bag on top of the things on the hall table. "What's wrong?"

It was the first time I'd ever called her Jake to her face but she didn't notice.

"Soph!" She scrambled to her feet. "Thank God you're here!"

She'd been looking for the bag of old pickle jars she'd left in the cupboard. "You haven't seen them, have you?"

"Pickle jars?" The day I'd cleaned out this same cupboard seemed to have happened about a hundred years ago, but I could still remember it. Clearly. I saw Barbee step over all the junk on her way out. I heard her say, "You know, my dad's taking stuff to the recycling place tomorrow if you want to get rid of some of this." I saw myself lug several bags of empty jars and bottles across the street.

"Why? Were they valuable?"

"You *have* seen them!" She was the bomb victim who thinks she sees her family limping towards her through the rubble. "Where did you put them?"

I knew what I was going to say wasn't what she wanted to hear, but I had to say it, didn't I?

"I gave them to Mr Scutari to take to the recycling place."

I'd never seen anyone literally *crumple* before.

"Oh my God!" She landed on a sign advertising shoe polish. "Are you sure? You didn't put them in the garden?"

"I'm really really sorry." I made some room among the boxes and sat down beside her. I put my arm round her. "I didn't know they were worth anything."

"They weren't." She leant her head against my shoulder. "They were my emergency bank account."

Jake considered any money she received from selling a sculpture made of old tins or cereal boxes

172

as an unexpected windfall – a bonus. So she hid it in one of the pickle jars so it wouldn't be spent.

"Then I'd have it. You know, for an emergency."

And now she had the emergency out of a nightmare. The Big El was not only increasing the rents on the shop and the house, but he was keeping her original deposit on the house because of the new floor he'd had to put in when Bart ate the hose to the washing machine and flooded the kitchen last spring. He wanted two months' rent at the new rate before he'd renew the lease.

"I had nearly four thousand dollars in that pickle jar. We were home free." She smiled ruefully. "Well, not free – but at least we could stay in our home."

I couldn't stop saying how sorry I was.

"It's all right." Jake sighed. "And so it goes..."

"Maybe Daddy could let you have the money – you know, as a loan."

She shook her head. "'Neither a borrower, nor a lender be...'"

"Well, what if you explain to the landlord? What if I explain? Surely if I tell him what happened he'll give you extra time. These are extenuating circumstances, after all."

"And you think he'd believe you?"

"Why not? It's the truth."

"Sometimes the truth is the hardest thing to believe." Jake got to her feet. "Anyway, even if he did believe you, that doesn't mean he'd see it our way. It's to his advantage not to believe us – he wants us out."

I stood up too and started passing her the things to put back in the cupboard. "He can't possibly be that unreasonable."

Jake laughed. "You haven't met the Big El, have you?"

"But he has to have a heart."

"He's a businessman, not an iguana."

"But there must be something—"

"It's not your fault, Soph." She gave me a hug. "This is my problem. I'll think of something."

The trouble, of course, was that it *was* my fault. If I'd minded my own business none of this would have happened.

In Daddy's novels someone always has what he calls "a dark night of the soul". He says it's the moment when a person understands the truth about herself. I'd never really understood what he meant before, but that night was so dark I might as well have been underground. I tossed and turned, engulfed in the truth about myself. The truth was pretty *awful*.

The Salamancas had welcomed me into their home as if I were as much a member of the family as Bart or Pancho Villa, while I had acted as if they were from another planet – and not a better one either. The Salamancas had treated me with generosity and patience, and in return I'd treated them as if they were some of the natives Columbus brought back to Europe to entertain Queen Isabella.

**174**

"For Pete's sake," grumbled Tampa. "Go to sleep, will you?"

But when I did fall asleep I dreamt that Jake, Tampa, Gallup, Bart, Pancho Villa, Bill and even Houdini had all been thrown out on the street. They were living in the doorway of the church up the road. It was winter and snow covered their cardboard box so that it looked like an igloo. They were all huddled together around a small fire. Bill's head poked out of Gallup's jacket and Bart was chewing on a corner of their pathetic shelter. Jake was toasting marshmallows.

"There must be *something* I can do!" I shouted in my dream.

Jake looked up with a smile. "Don't worry, Soph, you've done enough."

# I Finally Have a Good Idea

Jake talked to the Big El on Sunday, but the Big El wouldn't budge. Pay up or go, said the Big El.

"What'd I tell you?" said Jake. "His ancestors probably threw widows and orphans out in the snow."

"So now what?" I asked.

Mummy went into shock the time the credit card company made a mistake and she had her Visa card confiscated in Sainsbury's. She would have a migraine for the next six months if she were evicted, but Jake was philosophical.

"Now I guess I start looking for someplace we can afford."

That afternoon Bachman and I went to see the Celebrity Path in the botanical gardens. The names of all the famous people who were born in Brooklyn were embedded in the pavement.

There were more famous people born in Brooklyn than one would have thought (there

**176**

were definitely a lot more than *I* would have thought). F. Murray Abraham, Barbra Streisand, Phillip Lopate, Tony Lo Bianco, Beverly Pepper, Marty Glickman, Eubie Blake, Woody Allen, Joe Bologna, Fyvush Finkel, Julius La Rosa, Henny Youngman, Harvey Lichtenstein, Norman Mailer, Isaac Asimov... But I wasn't really paying much attention.

"Earth calling Sophie! Earth calling Sophie!" Bachman was waving his hand in front of my face. "What's wrong with you? That's Walt Whitman you're standing on."

"Who?"

"Walt Whitman. Arguably the greatest American poet. He's definitely the greatest American gay poet."

I apologized. "I'm sort of distracted. Perhaps I should go home. I'm not much company today."

"You gonna tell me what's wrong?"

I've always been taught that private family matters are private family matters, and that one doesn't blab them to people not in the family. This has always been a golden rule in our house. Every ancestor I'd ever had would be rolling round in their grave if I told Bachman the truth.

"It's Jake." It was more a sob than a statement. "She's being evicted. And it's all my fault."

We sat on a bench while I told him what had happened. It took a while because I couldn't stop crying.

"Tone it down, will you?" whispered Bachman.

177

"Everybody's looking at us. They'll think I'm making you cry."

For once in my life I didn't care who was looking at me. "Jake's been nothing but good to me," I gurgled. "And how do I repay her? I get her thrown out of her home."

Bachman tried to comfort me. "You're getting yourself all worked up about nothing. Jake's right, Soph. It's not your fault; it was an accident."

"It's too bad I didn't really have an accident. If I'd fallen because of that railing then we could have sued the Big El and Jake wouldn't have to move."

"Well, you didn't." He handed me a bandanna from his pocket. "And it's too late now."

I blew my nose. And at the same time I blew away the clouds that clogged my brain. "Oh my God!" I practically shook Bachman, I was so excited. "That's it! Bobby, you're a genius! That's the solution to everything."

He looked at me as though I'd lost my mind. "What is? Blowing your nose?"

"No, you berk. Suing the Big El."

"You what? You're going to break your leg on purpose?"

"Of course not." I'd never really been a big fan of pain. "And besides, a broken leg wouldn't really do it, would it? I mean, it's not as if I'd lose time off work or my life for it. It has to be something much more dramatic."

"Like what? Throwing yourself in front of his car?"

I shook my head. "Too dodgy. I could really get hurt doing that." I'd stopped crying and was thinking hard. "It has to be something vague and hard to prove."

"You mean like whiplash? My grandmother got whiplash once. You couldn't see anything in the X-rays but she bought herself a condo in Florida with what she got from the insurance company."

Grandmother! Nana Bea! Of course! I'd never in a million years pictured myself embracing someone who looked like Bachman, but I threw my arms around him now. "You really are a genius!"

"I don't think you can get whiplash falling off a stoop."

"But what if I hurt my back? If I did something to my back it could mess me up for the rest of my life."

"You're going to break your back?"

I smiled like a pig that's just eaten a pair of sunglasses. "No. I'm just going to act like I have."

"But you can't do that. Like you said before, what if you really hurt yourself?"

"But that's the point. I'm not going to. The whole thing's going to be staged. Like in a film."

Bachman still wasn't convinced. "I don't know if you can sue him—"

"Of course I can. This is America, remember? Litigation's your favourite indoor sport."

"Get a grip on the wheel, Soph. Do you know how long it takes to sue someone? You're only going to be here a couple more weeks."

"But that's the beauty of it. I'm not really going to sue him."

"You're not?"

"Of course not. I'm just going to threaten him. You know, as a bargaining tool. So Jake has something to negotiate with. That's what she said she needed. Something to hold over him."

He cocked his head to one side, pressing his lips together. "I don't know... Maybe you oughta think it over. See how you feel tomorrow."

Thinking it over was something I knew I shouldn't do. If I thought it over, all the things that could go wrong – and all the reasons why it was a really bad idea – were bound to occur to me. By the morning I'd almost certainly feel that I was losing my mind.

I held out my hand. "Give me your phone, Bachman. Please."

"What for?"

"I want to ring Barbee."

"What for?"

"Are we in a valley or something? It sounds like there's an echo."

"What do you want the phone for?"

"I'm going to need all the witnesses I can get."

# Move Over, Julia Roberts

Despite the fact that the only time I'd ever been on stage was the Christmas play in primary school (when I was so nervous that instead of saying, "We come bearing gifts for the Son of God", I said, "We come with bears for the sun god"), my performance was flawless.

Bachman directed ("Woody Allen isn't the only director born in Brooklyn," he said). Our timing was perfect. We strolled round the corner; we waved to Barbee and Will on the steps of the Scutaris'; we chatted as we came down Herkimer Street, two teenagers without a care in the world. And then *disaster struck*. I stumbled on the pavement in front of the Casa Salamanca (much as I always did). I let out a shriek of surprise as I lurched past Bachman. Acting as if he was trying to grab me, Bachman held me steady while I took hold of the handrail. There was the sound of splitting wood, and the railing and I (supple and flexible thanks to my yoga practice) flew back-wards. Bachman caught me and brought us both to the ground.

Our audience (all four Scutaris and two Casa-mayors) was one that any actor would kill for. They were on their feet before we hit the ground, shouting, "Soph! Soph! Are you all right?"

But no one was shouting more loudly than I was.

"My back!" I howled. "My back! My back!"

Jake came flying through the front door faster than a speeding bullet.

"Don't move her!" she was screaming. "Sophie, honey, just stay where you are."

I groaned. "I'm *so* sorry. Now look what I've done."

"That's what I like about you people," said Jake as she threw herself down beside me. "You always apologize when you haven't done anything wrong."

It was definitely the performance of a lifetime. I didn't become hysterical or overact. I kept my upper lip stiff. I was quiet with the incredible pain – and more concerned for the trouble I was caus-ing than the fact that I might be scarred for life by my terrible ordeal.

"Stop being so English," ordered Jake. "If you want to scream, scream."

I smiled weakly and said I thought I could bear it.

I was taken the few blocks to the hospital in an ambulance. Thank God Mummy had me insured.

Bachman stayed with Gallup and Tampa, and Jake came with me, holding my hand and telling me a story about a friend of hers who tripped getting out of a car and ended up in traction – presumably to reassure me that everything would be all right. I moaned gently the whole time and tried to look brave.

The doctor said the X-rays showed that nothing was broken, but that, judging by my symptoms, I might have done some damage to my spine. The doctor said that backs could be tricky.

"Really?" I said in a small voice tight with pain.

We were ages in Emergency, of course, but when we got back to the Casa Salamanca the Scutaris were all still on their porch, waiting. George carried me into the house.

"Put her in my room," ordered Jake.

"Oh, no," I protested. "I don't want to put you out. I'll be fine on the floor."

Jake told me not to be ridiculous. "We can't have you sharing with Tampa in your condition. You need your rest. I'll sleep on the army cot in the living room."

Mr Scutari brought one of the Scutari portable tellies over (they had five) and put it in my room. "Take your mind off the agony," said Mr Scutari, who had back trouble of his own.

We all had supper in my room that night, including Bachman and Barbee.

We'd just finished eating when Jake suddenly slapped her forehead. "I don't believe it!" she cried. "With all the excitement we forgot to call your mom."

I didn't particularly want to get Caroline Pitt-Turnbull involved in this drama just yet. If she thought I really was injured she might do something rash. Like come over herself to see how I was or even take me home.

"It can wait till tomorrow," I said quickly. "I'm sure I'll feel better by then. I don't want to worry her needlessly."

Casually – as though it had only just occurred to him – Bachman said, "You know, there's someone else you forgot to call."

Jake blinked. "There is?"

"Yeah." Bachman started gathering up the plates. "Shouldn't you call the Big El?"

Jake blinked again. The trauma of finding her house guest in a crumpled heap on the pavement had obviously driven all thoughts of the landlord from her mind. "The Big El?"

"Yeah." Bachman nodded. "I mean, it's his fault, isn't it? If that railing didn't give way Soph wouldn't've gone down like a bison shot at close range."

"But the X-rays..." mumbled Jake.

"Doesn't matter," he said. "The doctor said she'd messed up her back, didn't he? That kind of thing can be with you all your life."

Jake looked stricken. This hadn't occurred to her either. "But we'd have to prove—"

"You've got witnesses," chimed in Barbee.

"Not just me and Will, but my mom and dad, and the boys too."

"And me," said Bachman. "And the broken railing."

Jake looked at her watch. "It's kind of late. Do you think I should call him now?"

I stifled a groan of pain. "No, leave it," I gasped. "I really hate to be a nuisance."

Bachman and Barbee said, "Yeah. Call him now."

Jake went off to ring the Big El, with Tampa and Gallup clamouring behind her.

As soon as the door closed behind them, Barbee collapsed on the bed. "This is *so great*!" she shrieked. "I've never done anything this exciting in my life."

"Me neither." Bachman plonked himself down on the other side. "I feel like Batman or something – righting wrongs ... seeing justice is done..."

"Didn't I tell you it would work?" If I hadn't been afraid of getting caught I might have danced around the room.

"We're not clear yet, though," said Bachman. "This is only phase one. There's still the Big El to deal with."

The new Sophie Pitt-Turnbull laughed. "Don't worry about him. The Big El will be easy-peasy."

# Home Again, Home Again,
## Jiggety-Jig

I was in bed for the next four days. This may sound like a less than brilliant way to spend some of the few remaining days of one's holiday, but it really wasn't so bad.

Tampa moved into Jake's room to keep me company, and Gallup, Bart and Pancho Villa spent most of their days up there too, mainly playing cards and board games – with special visits from Bill. Barbee and Will came over at noon to make us all lunch, and then they'd usually hang out with us till Jake got home from the shop. Bachman took the evening shift.

The Big El came by on Monday, talked to Jake on the phone on Tuesday, and came round again on Wednesday. He was a small man in a wrinkled summer suit whose forehead perspired so much it looked like it might melt. On Monday he brought flowers and a man to fix the stairs.

"How're you doing?" he wanted to know.

Jake stood behind him with her arms folded in front of her, making faces.

I adjusted my accent a bit so it sounded as though I was related to the Queen. "Except for the fact that I can't move without the most astonishing pain, I'm fine, thank you."

The Big El rocked back and forth on his heels. "So what's the doc say? You going to be OK?"

"It's too early to tell." I could smile like the Queen too. "Backs, you know. They can be tricky."

"You should've had the stoop repaired before someone got hurt," said Jake. "Like I told you."

"It's lucky my uncle's a solicitor," I said, which actually is the truth. "I'm sure he must have colleagues in New York."

The Big El looked at Jake.

She could smile like the Queen too. "Lawyer," she translated.

The Big El rocked some more. "Oh, I don't think there'll be any need for lawyers..." he mumbled.

I said I hoped not and winced in pain.

On Tuesday night he and Jake had a long conversation on the phone. She told him she felt my recovery was being hampered by the fact that I was worried she and her children were going to be made homeless. The Big El accused her of trying to blackmail him. Jake said, "I'm not trying to blackmail you. I'm just trying to give you some useful information. Like when I told you to fix the stoop."

On Wednesday the Big El came round with a

**187**

new lease – two years at the old rent, and he was forgetting about the deposit.

I thought it best to stay in bed another day so Jake wouldn't get suspicious, but on Friday I came down to breakfast whistling.

"You're walking!" Jake hugged me so hard it was a wonder she didn't do me an injury.

I said I was feeling much better.

"Cool!" exclaimed Tampa. "Now we can go to the park."

My bag arrived on Saturday morning.

"If only it could talk," said Jake. "I'd sure love to know where it's been."

Since I only had another week it didn't seem worth the bother to unpack it, so I opened it to take out Bunny, who wanted to stay with Tampa, and then I shut it again. I reckoned I could put all my new stuff in a cardboard box. I doubted the airline would lose that.

My flight back to England wasn't until nearly ten on my last night, so we had a barbecue in the garden before I left. Bachman came, of course, and the Scutaris, and Melody from the shop and her boyfriend came as well. The Scutaris gave me a Brooklyn T-shirt and matching baseball cap as a going-away present.

"So you don't forget us," said Mrs Scutari.

I said I didn't think that was likely.

I had such a good time that I found myself telling them all the story of my trip up Flatbush

188

Avenue to get a fan. There were tears in Jake's eyes, she was laughing so much.

"I'll say one thing for you Brits," said Mr Scutari, "you're feisty, that's for sure."

"You don't know the half of it," said Bachman.

Barbee and Bachman came with us to the airport. Barbee started crying the second we walked into the terminal.

"It's just that I'm going to miss you," she kept saying. "This has been the best summer I've ever had."

I linked my arm through hers. "Me too."

Bachman gave her his bandanna.

By the time we had to say goodbye, everybody but Bachman was crying.

"You think you'll ever come back?" he asked.

I said I'd like to see anyone stop me.

# The New Me

Mummy and Daddy were waiting at Heathrow for me. I'd never noticed before how pale they are. Pale and rather bland. I waved, but they didn't wave back. They didn't actually see me until I was standing right in front of them.

"Good Lord, Sophie!" Mummy laughed. "Is that you?"

She looked positively *shocked*. *Shocked* as in she hadn't recognized her own daughter.

Daddy said, "Have you got taller?"

Mummy linked arms as we made our way to the car park. "Glad to be back?" she asked.

The honest answer to this was *sort of*. *Sort of* as in yes and no.

"I could murder a proper cup of tea."

"Does that mean you didn't miss us?" asked Daddy.

"Of course I missed you. You're my family."
But now I had another family on the other side

of the pond, and I was already starting to miss them.

"Jocelyn's been ringing you for days," said Mummy while we waited for Daddy to work out how to pay the parking ticket. "I told her when you were getting back, but she won't let up." She lowered her voice as though any of the families pushing mountains of luggage before them might be interested in Jocelyn Scolfield. "Just between you and me, I think she may have suffered a broken heart this summer."

"Poor Jocelyn. What a way to spend your holiday."

The thing was, I meant it. I was too happy myself to feel like gloating. Among the dozens of things I'd learnt in the last six weeks was a new respect for life. Bad or good, lucky or unlucky, up or down, being alive was a pretty exciting thing – so long as you didn't sit in the house watching adverts all day and avoiding it.

"She's very anxious to speak to you," said Mummy.

"I'll ring her as soon as I've had my tea." I wasn't going to gloat, but I wasn't going to hold back on the summer I'd had either. "I'm anxious to speak to her too."